THE
LASCAUX PRIZE
VOL 5

THE
LASCAUX PRIZE
VOL 5

edited by
Camille Griep
Stephen Parrish
Wendy Russ

ISBN 10: 0-9851666-8-1
ISBN 13: 978-0-9851666-8-7

Cover design by Wendy Russ.
Cover art by Edward Robert Hughes: "The Valkyrie's Vigil," watercolor on paper, 1906.

Lascaux Books
www.lascauxbooks.com

Contents

continued next page

Poetry Finalists (continued)

Short Story Winner

Short Story Finalists

Introduction

The editors of *The Lascaux Review* spent a year culling thousands of submissions to assemble the seven flash pieces, sixteen poems, and seven short stories that appear in this volume. They constitute a powerful representation of what writers around the world have written over the last year.

When successful writers are asked how to become a good writer, the first answer they usually give is "Read." Second to that, the editors of this volume would argue that the most effective way to learn what works and what doesn't in fiction or poetry is to judge thousands of stories and poems, but admit not everyone has the opportunity. Creative writing teachers know good writers started as good readers. So do literary journal editors. Great writing stands out, and it's not always easy to say why.

We look for engaging narratives and beautiful language, of course, but we also hope to learn something, maybe even about ourselves. Once in a while a story or poem comes along that takes our breath away and sends us immediately back to the beginning to read it again. We trust you'll find a few such pieces in this anthology.

We'd like to thank all the contributors as well as those who shared their work but didn't make it into the book; we appreciated everyone's effort and enjoyed being provided a broad view of the literary landscape. Thanks also to Angela Kubinec who assisted with the reading. Our purpose in this volume has been the same as in those preceding it: to discover quality writing, to acknowledge it, to bring it to light.

Camille Griep
Stephen Parrish
Wendy Russ

Clemency

by Cady Vishniac

A dead ringer for Josey. She sneezes as she walks into the pharmacy, and I look up from the newspaper I'm not supposed to be reading. For a split second I think it's really her, but then I remember Josey's older now, way older than this girl. In my head I'm already rehearsing the story I'll tell my wife—you'd think it would be depressing, but we like to talk about her, about our daughter. Josey, I mean.

I manage to squeak out a "Welcome." Last week my boss said to greet the customers with genuine enthusiasm. A tall order, but I need the job if my wife and I are going to keep sending Ashyra—that's Josey's daughter—to Catholic school. "Welcome," I say again, my voice firmer.

Not-Josey sniffles. She coughs chunky phlegm right on-to her hand, and says, "Excuse me." Sickly. Probably using, and in that respect even more like my daughter. From the way she stands fingering the boxes of tissues, I'm aware she's about to steal. But I don't plan to stop her. If she can't afford anything to wipe her face with, well, she can't afford it. What kind of man would I be if I came between a sick young lady and some Kleenex? How could I look my wife and granddaughter in the eye?

I think of it like one of the problem-solving exercises Ashyra brings home from her teacher. There's a security camera pointed right at me. Corporate says the majority of theft is committed by employees, or with employee consent, and I suppose that's true. So I'm looking for a way I can consent to let not-Josey walk out with the tissues. The catch is I don't want to be fired.

What I come up with is I'll go to the frozen self-checkout station and see if I can coax the computer to life for the fifth time today. While I'm busy, not-Josey can grab her tissues. Later, if anybody checks the footage, all they'll see is me being a good worker, and I'll be able to tell my wife about it, about how clever I was, which is a bonus.

So I spend the next twenty minutes kneeling on the floor plugging and unplugging the machine. It's not a huge deal because nobody else comes in. I hear not-Josey wander through our aisles, stealing the tissues along with a week's worth of groceries. Also hacking up a lung.

"Excuse me," she says about the hacking.

"Piece of shit," I say about the checkout.

And then she walks out and the bell rings and the door squeaks and she sniffles one last time and mutters, "Have a good day," which is maybe as close as she can come to thanks. I don't look up. It's complicated, like any grief. I do want to tell my wife later but just now, I don't want to see the girl's face, which is my daughter's face. I don't want to see at all.

Marriage Counseling
by Jackleen Holton

In the Hundred Years War, French soldiers set out to capture the English longbowmen, and when they caught
them, they chopped off their first two fingers. But those
archers who evaded capture, upon seeing the enemy's uniforms, would hold up index and middle finger in defiance
as if to say *I still got me fingers*. My husband, half Irish, half
Brummie, told me this story on the motorway between
Birmingham and London after some knob jockey cut us off.
Back home, I find it endearing when he flashes what my
yoga teacher refers to as *peace fingers* to unknowing American motorists, the captain cocks of the I-5. We watch *Peaky
Blinders*, a series set in the Midlands where he was born, the
Black Country, after the Great War a hundred years ago
when coal dust fell like snow on lamp-lit cobblestones. *Quit
your fuckin' whingin'*, yells a gangster as he slashes an ad-
versary across the face. *Quit your fuckin' whingin'*, says my
husband as I cry in the kitchen over the cutting board.
Then he laughs at me because I'm wearing a lilac yoga tank
with a lotus flower and the word *Bliss*. I bought him a book

called *Non-Violent Communication.* Now when he remembers, he tries to observe without judgment, share his feelings, state his needs, and make requests, but mostly he just shouts *I'm not fuckin' being violent.* In the parking lot after our counseling session, crows convene on a high wire, black against gray. He says *I think we're doing better,* holds a cigarette between his peace fingers. We kiss and walk to our separate cars. At the intersection, I watch my diamond ring pick up the sparse light from the sunroof, make tiny rainbows on the steering wheel. I'm startled by a honk. He holds up his middle finger, grinning. I come back with two, wiggle them like the legs of an upside-down stripper. He gets the green arrow, veers left. A smattering of blackbirds rise from a eucalyptus like ashes, swirl up into a smoke-stack-colored sky as I wait for a break in traffic to turn right.

A Tragedy, A Process, An Adjustment
by Betsy Porter

Did you pay the gas bill, he says: a sentence, not a question. *The lampshade is dusty.* And, *where'd you put the car keys?*

He is always surprising her with his dissatisfaction. One time, he comes home from work to find her drinking a glass of wine and his mouth turns down.

"What?" she says. From the corner of her eye, she sees her own hand loosely touching the stem of the glass, her bare thighs in the pajama shorts she wears to bed: all her guilty body.

"Mind if *I* have a glass?" he says, looking from her to the wine bottle, from the wine bottle to her.

"Of course not," she says. It's her first glass, her first few sips. The baby lies in her arm, sleeping. It's like he's asking some other question.

The cupboard door rasps, the glass clinks and because she's not looking, his irritation bounces off her, it glances off her and falls harmlessly elsewhere, like a wasted superpower. "Baby," she's saying. "Baby, baby." She risks waking

5

the child for no real reason. She clucks and bounces her until the girl raises her tiny fists in defense.

The cork pops and when she looks up, he is pouring, his movements exaggerated and precise—it's cupboard, glass, uncork, pouring—as if this were some kind of demonstration.

"It would be nice if you put out a glass for me, too."

"Just the glass?" she says stupidly, because she doesn't completely understand. "The empty glass."

"So I could have some, too. Is that too much to ask?" And he has that cordial smile.

"Why is this such a big deal?" she says. "Can't you just take out a glass? It takes like two seconds. You weren't here. I didn't know if you were *going* to be here, for dinner."

"Well, here I am," he says and spreads his arms. There he is. He is squinting his eyes like she's someone he might recognize.

*

She would be devastated if something happened to him—a car accident, for example, it's entirely possible. The road winds through the trees, and he works hard, to the point of exhaustion. There's sliding and darkness. Deer. Even, sometimes, ice. The thought comes to her from nowhere, when she's washing up after her dinner, it drops on her like a high, heavy weight. She has to stop and put the plate back in the sink before she drops it. She's oppressed by the strangeness of his absence, though he's sitting right there, at the table, still eating. Without turning, she sees him reflected in the window. The kitchen is smelling like carrot baby food and stew, familiar and comforting—a little soiled, like diapers. There are beads of moisture and her reflection in the window. Stuffy. He's always turning up the heat.

They would send a sheriff to tell her. After that, she can't imagine, who could imagine? She would be on her own without even having chosen that. It would be a tragedy, a process, an adjustment. It would be something that just happened, to her.

The heat pump still needs to be serviced. At any moment, that's what he'll be saying.

Eric. She turns her head to look at him—her husband—over the kitchen table. He is eating broccoli, cutting it with his knife. He is lifting the little trees up to his face with the fork.

"A Tragedy, A Process, An Adjustment" was originally performed by Liars' League.

Prologue
by Michelle Ross

My mother was the girl who pushed the witch into the oven, only it wasn't quite like you've heard. She entered the witch's house alone. Her siblings—there were four of them—weren't survivors. When their parents left them by that fire deep in the woods, the first child climbed a tree and wrapped herself in a cocoon she would never emerge from; the second chopped wood for hours on end until, his vision blurry, he mistook his legs for logs and bled out in intricate rivulets; the third buried himself beside a poison ivy, and the ivy crept spider-like along the forest floor; the fourth submerged herself in a murmuring lagoon.

My mother wasn't fooled by the bread walls, the cake roof, the window panes made of sugar. She knew that sweetness was often a trick.

But always, she took what she could get.

You know what happened next. The witch took her in, gave her free rein of the pantry.

What you might not know is that life with the witch was not all bad. There was food aplenty; a warm, soft place to sleep. In the evenings, they sat by the hearth and told stories.

For her room and board, my mother had chores, and yes, the witch was sometimes on her back. My mother kneaded the dough too roughly; she swept the floors too harshly; she clanked the dishes too loudly. But, my mother conceded, the witch's criticisms were not unjust. My mother never was much of a homemaker.

This business about the oven, my mother didn't see it coming. Sure, the witch remarked on the fit of her clothes, the curves of her flesh. What woman didn't assess the bodies of the girls in her care? And the witch, she couldn't have been more lovely about it—never a cruel word, only flattery. It wasn't until the witch instructed her one day to stick her head inside the oven to check that it was hot that my mother gleaned she'd been duped. My mother nursed her broken heart by sucking severed pieces of sugar window pane while the witch's scream dwindled in the fire.

The part my mother didn't tell me, the part I know without a doubt to be true, is that she trusted no one thereafter. Yet she married and gave birth to a daughter of her own.

"Prologue" originally appeared in *Gravel*.

Shirt Eater
by Kari Shemwell

This is one gesture of love I have received: In the back seat of a rental car, while driving across the border, you, the man with whom I am having my very first affair, try to eat my shirt.

The yoga instructor from California drives stick through the mountains towards the airport. She gave us each a pink stone the day we met her, rose quartz, told us to tape it to our chests to absorb stress and open our hearts. In bed last night, our final evening together, you peeled the translucent stone from my skin and gave me yours, said, don't tell. The yoga instructor has also given us drugs. The college girl next to me is blazing behind her silk scarf, tracing her tattoos with her fingers, and the beach-town musician riding shotgun hasn't stopped singing since the city. You and I are shoulder to shoulder, melting. Through the windows, we all point at ruined buildings, castles maybe, that decorate the hillsides. Until now, I've never admitted that anything could be so old.

In your hotel room this morning I woke to news of another gun massacre back home, and you asked me, do Americans even feel it anymore, sorrow? You said, perhaps a language barrier divides us.

You came here on holiday to meet with secondary school friends. Me, I'd just grown angry, at twenty-seven, by the thought of being young. We've drank so much my left kidney spasms each morning before breakfast. This is what young people do. We found the others along the way. The musician, who we encountered eating mushrooms in a cable car over the Alps, admitted that he had planned to kill himself back in Arizona but, in a last ditch effort, decided to cross the pond, instead. We found the yoga instructor dodging visa requirements in Portugal. She'd heard rumors of a center of energy in the mountains and was teaching the college girl to feel for it in the ground. And you and I discovered each other alone on the street at night, each unearthing just how late we could stay up. You told me, I've never thought of cheating before, and I said, I'm afraid of disappearing.

Now it's time to for you to go home to your wife. In the rental car on the way to the airport you are substance-lit, desperate, like you were that first night when we stayed up until dawn. I told you, I'm too young to be a wife, and you begged me to please just lie naked in your bed, said you needed to see me, that you wouldn't touch unless I asked. I undressed and sat on the edge. You watched from the chair in the corner like I was a movie, and finally whispered, Jesus.

When I left early in the morning, you said, at least we didn't sleep together, and I said, I think what we did was worse.

The next night, I asked you to touch me.

Now, in the back seat, you have that same begging look, as if your life will end when we arrive at the airport, like it's your last supper and you aren't ready to die yet.

You look at me, staring again, then press your thumb to my lips. You say, I'm going to bite your shirt, is it expensive?

What? I ask, but you press my lips harder, release, then grab the shoulder of my shirt with your teeth and pull.

Stop, I say, laughing at first.

But you won't stop. Your face is wild. You tug at the shirt until it stretches off my shoulder and the edge of the short sleeve cuts into the skin on the underside of my arm.

Stop, I say again, you're hurting me.

Just yesterday we went to visit one of Europe's oldest institutes of science. You took me, alone, into the tower of the observatory and asked to fuck me against the curved stone wall. I said, I can't, I'm American and we don't do PDA.

You slid your hand under my skirt and touched me, said, but I'm not, and you're not in America anymore.

Now, the college girl screams and pulls me toward her, but you won't let go of my sleeve—savage, shaking your head like an animal tearing at a scrap of flesh.

The yoga instructor yells your name from the driver's seat, demanding that you release me, open your mouth. The musician stops singing and swats at you with an empty soda bottle.

Finally, the fabric rips open. I fall back into the college girl's arms. We all stare at you, wondering what you might do next. A jagged square of cloth hangs from your lips. You pull the tattered fabric into your mouth, chewing.

No one speaks again for most of the drive, and I suddenly realize what you and I have done, how we've been striking matches in the forest during a drought. My shirt hangs from my shoulder, split. You take my hand. You say to no one in particular, Americans spill all their secrets.

When we arrive at the airport, you can hardly stand. We wait in the parking lot with your bags while you go into the restroom. You return with your phone pressed to your ear, talking to your wife, saying, I'm not coming home, I'm sorry.

The musician runs to you, yanks the phone from your hand, says, whoa buddy.

You lose your balance and stumble, crumpling like a paper ball onto the blacktop.

The yoga instructor puts her hands on your chest, pats your face, says, hey there, what are you doing? Says, two hours ago, when you were sober, you were getting on that plane. Says, think about this.

You only look up at me from the pavement, waiting for me to say one word: Stay.

But my sleeve is ripped, my skin carpet-burned, and you're part fabric now.

A Mystery
by K. J. Stevens

When Sadie appears in the kitchen, I'm sprucing up my drink. More V8. More Absolut. Another Asiago stuffed olive.

"Daddy, there's another one out there."

Her red hair is all frizzy. Pajamas buttoned off-kilter. She's wearing one orange sock and one green.

"Another what?" I ask.

"Another bunny. It's on the front step."

I sip my drink. She rubs her eyes.

"Why does he keep doing that?" she asks.

"It's what they do, honey. Cats hunt."

"Why can't he just eat cat food?"

I hand her a piece of thick, sweet-smoked bacon. Just the thing to take our minds off the cat and bunnies and death.

"Delicious!" she says. "And eggs?"

I remove the lid from the pan. Yolks for me, scrambled for her.

"Good job, Daddy!"

At the table, we scrape forks around on our plates and nibble bacon and toast. Sadie slurps OJ through a curly straw. The empty chair between us creates an awful silence. I finish my drink. Get up to make another.

It's odd living this new life so far from the city. Our home is an old parsonage on two acres and there is a small church next door. We are renovating it. Transforming it from an abandoned house of worship into a bright, colorful space for reading and writing and painting. Yet, there's lots to do.

Sadie's adjusting well to the move and this surprises me. Not only has she been uprooted from home and school, but she's also the one that found her—my wife, her mother—naked in the bathroom. Curled up between the toilet and tub. Blood pouring out the back of her head.

Sadie sets aside her fork. Slides her plate away.

"But why does he kill the babies?"

"Some things are a mystery," I say.

*

An hour later, Sadie's on the deck, coloring.

"Chester!" she calls, "Here kitty!"

Chester's been hunting for a month. We only catch glimpses of him. A flash of gray darting through grass. A shadow sneaking through bushes. A tail twitching in the trees. Besides these fleeting moments, the only real signs we have of Chester are the trophies he leaves behind.

At first, there were feathers under the deck. A dead field mouse on the doorstep. Then a robin, a dove, a ground squirrel, a mole. Now, he has found the bunny hole.

I drink and watch Sadie and go through the list in my head. *Refinish the deck. Mow the lawn. Repaint the church.*

Shingle the steeple. But I'll get none of it done because today may be the day Maggie wakes. Instead of working, we'll drive to Thunder Bay General Hospital. Sit in Maggie's room, turn on the TV, and watch SpongeBob until lunchtime when we walk to Gepetto's. Sadie will order Cleo's fancy fish sticks and mashed potatoes. I'll get the Figaro double-bacon cheeseburger. When the check comes, Sadie will insist that the waitress *box up the leftovers for Mom.*

We'll take the Styrofoam box to the hospital. Nurse Nancy will promise to put the food in the refrigerator for safe-keeping.

Our visit will last well into the afternoon. There'll be more TV. Lots of chatting. Then finally, we'll read a book. Whatever Sadie's brought. And for a short while, we aren't just biding time with a body in a bed fed by bagged fluids, relieved by tubes, and healing in medicated sleep. We are a family. Husband and wife and daughter, on the cusp of great things.

I mix a drink. Take a shoe box from Maggie's closet. Put on gloves and head for the door. I expect something grue-some, like the others. One found in the driveway, its head nearly torn from its body. Another in the front yard miss-ing its front legs and patches of fur. But when I open the door, the bunny isn't on the step as Sadie's said. It's under the rosebush a few feet away. Unlike the others, this one looks good. No blood. No missing limbs or missing fur. I hear Sadie coming, so I scoop up the bunny and plop it into the box. Its body makes a gurgling sound.

"Funeral time?" Sadie asks.

I close the lid. Take another drink.

"It's time," I say.

We walk into the church and I place the box atop the altar, under a big wooden cross that hangs on the wall. We sit in the front pew side by side.

"What should we say this time?" I ask.

I'm at the bottom of my glass. Rattling ice cubes.

Sadie picks up a Bible. Thumbs through the pages.

"I'll find something," she says.

*

We sit silently in warm light that slants through the tall stained glass windows. Flies buzz near the ceiling and there is something in the attic—a mouse, probably—and I consider leaving the church door open when we leave so that Chester can do some hunting.

"Here, Daddy," she says, and she hands me the book. "Read this one."

Her little finger points to one single line.

"Behold, I shew you a mystery; We shall not all sleep, but we shall all be changed."

I close the book. We sit and stare at the cross. And from atop the altar, inside the shoe box, comes the most delicate scratching sound.

Crossing

by Vickie Weaver

The three a.m. call. A murder/suicide situation. This is a not uncommon occurrence with elderly couples, I am told.

I should drive fast because one of them is whispering in an ER cubicle.

A train's full-bodied horn warns its approach. Red lights blare. The crossing arms are just down; for half a breath I consider weaving through.

Hindsight arrives. I could not have made it.

The train glides fast. Rails yield with each set of boxcar wheels. pulsepulse. pulsepulse. I close my eyes against the dizziness of travel through time and space.

Mom smoked Pall Malls like it was her job. In my youth, she sat at the kitchen dinette and penciled budgets with categories such as *groc, cig, rent*, and *lights* on the backs of used envelopes. Her gloveless hands pinned our sheets on the line in winter. Things did get better, but not better enough to make her forget that she could have chosen someone else.

Dad was the one all of us obeyed. On his day off, we waited in the Plymouth, at the curb, while he drank at the bar. He kept his Bible in the trunk where the spare should have been. On autumn nights, he signaled UFOs with a flashlight, and carried paranoia with him everywhere, a fat tick on his scalp.

I open my eyes to the quiet; the road is open.

It doesn't matter if it's mom or dad. The end is the same. I don't want to meet the eyes of medical personnel who will expect me to wail while we peer into the immediate future. I want to travel a journey of imagination that I alone steer while I sit with a fountain Coke, biting ice, in the hospital cafeteria.

Foal

by Lois P. Jones

In your next life you will be
birthed in needles
of hoarfrost, your eyes still
in the blue gauze between

this world and the next
and I will kneel so close
you will smell the hot iron
waiting to singe

your skin. You'll hear
the crackle of the flame
and your throat will prickle
with stars. I'll wrap your shins

in nettle and this shelter will fall
deeply into zero. This is the start
of your suffering for the children,
yours who became

the wanderers, beaten between
the withers, broken and unridable
in the world's dark loam. There is
no animal to save you now

no purling stream to fold
shame into, not even the jackdaw
as witness, or a single crofter
awake in this cat's eye hour.

Revenge tries on its black
bridle then drapes it over
the swinging fence.
Father, I will not take out

your eyes but I will brand you
with the word you fear
and you will wear it
and you will wear it

and give up everything to winter.

"Foal" also won the Bristol Poetry Prize.

Girl Unforgotten

by Anna Bernstein

Who put Bella in the Wych elm?
—Graffiti repeated around Hagley woods following the discovery of a local sex worker's body inside a tree.

B ella, the question is not
 who put you in the elm. The question is
who marred the town with looping
phrases of the first place of your rest,
love letters, in a sense, to your
wronged body, to your eyes
closed against the inner bark of the tree,
soft as antler velvet: the bark, your eyes.
One hand was flung above you
like a dancer and the other thrown
into the ground five violent feet away
from you. And boys woke up early to
help their mothers with breakfast,
run laps in fields, scrawl your name
on buildings, by train tracks, on

obelisks, in heady lines of black.
Agape at an old mystery,
they claimed it for themselves in
shivering night air with
can of paint in hand, felt pleasantly
an unexpected anger for you
that they reined in
before sadness. They prefer
to remember you
as a dancer; they prefer
to remember you
as a god. And when they
take their girls to
prom, they will watch the
translucent sheen rising off
silk dresses, the delicate meshes
across shoulders, and they
will smile to the girls, fix
corsages to their wrists, and think
only of the taffeta
in your throat.

My Parents Jitterbug at Weddings
by Bethany Bowman

But most often slow dance on tired linoleum
those rare nights she bakes pies from rhubarb
neighbor kids haven't already ravaged with sugar.

My parents jitterbug at weddings, but most often
swat mosquitoes on cool pavement, watch yellow
moonflowers open in the green space by the garage.

My parents jitterbug at weddings, but most often
Dad's cutting across the cemetery to mow around
the gingko biloba that brings some cheer to my

grandmother's evening years. He'll try not to stew
about the jerk from his plant who won't let him
read on his lunch, try not to pick dead petals

off the dead's geraniums as Mom plays back
half a dozen messages: a cousin requests a ride,
church divorcee, prayer, cafeteria lady, piano.

Maybe one day, a snippet from her eldest—
nothing profound—a simple thank you in the form
of a poem that will do nothing to ease the pain

of living three states away from her only grandkids,
but she'll pin it to the fridge with her "dry crust of bread"
magnet, assure friends it's not meant to be profane.

My parents jitterbug at weddings, but most often
hold hands to say grace, which they insist
cannot be earned, as they toil, wait, and let go.

Serving

by Kari Gunter-Seymour

Remember that time your dog died
and I didn't tell you for months because
you had deployed and George Bush
was shouting, *Bring it on,* and we were all
thinking that Korea was fixing to blow.
But when I emailed to say we were headed
for West Virginia, you fired back,
Mom, where is Annie? and I had to say
she was hit by a car. I sent brownies loaded
with black walnuts from the old home place.

Or when you called me from Iraq asking
me to talk to people about donating shoes
and I told you it was hopeless because
of the Tsunami, everyone was already donating.
You said *Hell with that* and your unit threw

in their paychecks and bought all those families
just outside Fallujah new shoes off the Internet.
I made two hundred popcorn balls
wrapped in wax paper.

Or that February you came home for R&R,
so sad and sick. I baked your favorite, meatloaf,
and you said you couldn't possibly, but I gave
you doe-eyes so you ate and threw up all night,
into the next day, saying over and over
Sweet Jesus, please, make it stop and I knew
you weren't talking about the meatloaf.

Or the day after Sergeant Crabtree went to Vegas
and blew his head off in the hotel bathroom,
while here at home your best friend got arrested
for selling narcotics and you said neither one
of them needed to and maybe wouldn't have
if you'd been there. So I shipped molasses cookies
thick with Crisco frosting, all the way to Kandahar.

Or the afternoon your farm boy fingers
tried to clamp the artery on that precious
baby girl, near the valley of Arghandab,
while her father screamed for Allah
and blood soaked your uniform
when you hugged her to you as she passed.
I drenched that fruitcake in brandy for three days.

But mostly it was the night your daughter was born
and we locked eyes across the birthing room.
I thought to myself, skillet-fried chicken
with candied sweet potatoes, fried okra,
lima beans with bacon, cornbread
and aunt Margaret's hot fudge cake.
We used the good dishes
and grandpa Oris said the blessing.

"Serving" originally appeared in *Still: The Journal.*

The Whole Pie

by Maurine Haltiner

I'm from cypher world—
Texas Department of Criminal
Justice, #3766612, cell 54B (bottom bunk), state-owned
property. I screwed up
in this Lone (some) Star State. I'm from robbery

gone awry (2nd degree felony), from falling
apart—a bit off-(meds)-kilter for a week or so—schiz-o-
phren-ic. I'm from being handcuffed after
drowning in my own gene pool.

I'm from two cellmates, repelling
magnets, *hands-off* the word. I'm from seven
weekly bars of soap, Sweet 'n Low-size, for
showers and sink-bunk-desk-(down-on-the-knees-floor)
scrubs. (God, help me, I pray.)

I'm from nixing a drug test when pissed
(passed) out like a racehorse, not a molecule
(miracle) left. I'm from parole

out of question this year, but trying
to be heart ready for steady walk away
on 27 March, 2026—a Friday, for sure.

I hear Plath's poems barking
off dog-eared pages. I understand Dickens, Steinbeck,
the well of Emerson's mind, Thoreau's Walden
roundabout. I haven't missed

the personal irony of the *Oxford American Writer's Thesaurus*
(1087 pages, 300,000 synonyms, 10,000 anti-nyms).
I read Ayn Rand's ego-scrapes and *Ella Minnow Pea*
(every letter gone, me in lockdown).

I'm from *Four and Twenty Jailbirds
Baked in a Pie,* want to fly home
to see my father die.

I smell pancakes at 0400 hours. On a good day
they come with a quartered pear un-
balanced
like the absent moon.

"The Whole Pie" originally appeared in *Encore* by NFSPS, and in the
poet's second book of poetry, *Every Angle of Moonshine.*

Outside of the World

by Lois P. Jones

Suppose the rain fell and only one man saw its fate.
And fate lay down until the snow iced
and the world found a place for the next god

by the very nature of things, by the way the peach tree
takes on the sun even when it doesn't need it. The way
it holds it in its branches waiting for the moment

when a fruit will call it to its next life. Suppose the bird
that sits alone on the branch or the chair facing it
were the rain and the way it goes. Suppose the way

it goes was all a god could ever muster in a single hand
and that was the life he left you. Suppose you never leave
because arrival and departure

are a limp arm on an operating table, and when you left
the room you are still there with your secrets exposed.
Suppose a doctor is a preacher

with a knife and you have let your feathers fall
in a pattern of despair. Suppose this is the only way
you can live when your brother sits in a chair of iron.

Suppose he never really left you and the day began
with this wind in the branches and never ends.
And your fingers were the flame of a life

you were still living. Suppose the man you wanted
came to you as if you were a house built
just for sleeping. Suppose your house caught fire

and that you lived this way because it's the only way
you knew. Suppose the world kept spinning
on its white stem without need for plucking.

Even when it glistened like a ripe fruit
and all you could do was come back
and try again to taste it.

Holy Jesus Miracle Temple Ribs

by Karla K. Morton

Its name, in purple neon,
wrapped two sides of the restaurant.

We had to go in pairs—
one as lookout in the running car
with the doors locked,

the other bolting in with exact change
plus a two dollar tip
that we might make it out alive.

It was Avenue D in Fort Pierce—
what *60 Minutes* just proclaimed
as the *Crack Cocaine Capital of America.*

But what's a Texas girl to do,
freshly married, new to Florida—
husband's spots showing
three days into it all,

craving *real* barbeque—
not that nasty vinegar mix
I once returned to the counter,
accusing them of serving tuna fish.

I was twenty-one and rolling coins.
I was *not* to come home—
lying in the wedding bed I'd made,

clinging to my dowry
of one Doberman Pinscher,
four years of college debt,
and an awesome ability to make good gravy.

This place, a poor girl's miracle—
a little bit of home wrung from
rolled quarters, nickels and dimes;

sweet sticky ribs that made you groan
in secular pleasure,
that made you believe,
if just for one night
when your belly was full,

that maybe, just maybe,
this whole marriage thing *wasn't* a sham,
and that man driving next to you
cursing the traffic
could turn back into the man you dated,

and those sucked-clean bones
could prophesy from your paper plate
to proclaim a future
better than the one ulcering inside;

praying for salvation
every Thursday night

like Abraham—
his pork rib dagger
raised high,
stopped by an angel, mid swing.

Song of the Dunghill Beetles
by George Petty

My son is on the phone again from jail,
angry at being jostled by the cops
while pissing expressively in the street.
Each time he calls the wire clicks and shrieks
with song whose wave distorted riffs evoke
the acid fog of alleys coast to coast,
a serenade for radiated earth
beamed from the magic cave where he will paint
huge images of saber-tusked creatures
stalking the littered streets in suit and tie,
that he and other beetle warriors
bite and slaughter, leave to fossilize,
returning to their dunghill for a feast.
But at the end instead of victory
his lyric turns to sobs and sentiment,
longing for the world it sang away,
as if the rubbled streets led home again.
The sappy show biz ending's all for me,

not the real him; when he starts that I quit.
He wouldn't sing that verse among his friends
huddled in the I-5 culvert cave,
lulled by the hum of trucks, the dripping rain.

Respire

by Karen Pojmann

When I stop to see you
and find in your place the husk
of a cyborg, the machine part
still forcing air into the part
that was you (a rude
overinflation), I go along with it.
Your family is there, so I pretend you
are there, in the middle of the room,
in the whoosh and clank,
though all your life you never
took such a deep breath.

Vertigo at Wolf Gap
by Jessamine Price

—To a friend in transition F2M

Back of the mountain, where the laurel grows,
we pitched our tent on the rocks above the gap
and built our fire by a valley like an ancient sea,
dark and hollow as the inside of God's ear.

Above us hang the mansions of the sky,
pulling gently with a drowning touch—
those dizzy-easy reefs of stars always drag me dropping—

But you can sit fine-balanced on the edge,
make the margined cliff your resting stillness,
jaunty as a fiddler focused
on the tender turnings of a jig,

the falling emptiness
a stage for distant watchings I can't see,
a path to stranger turnings no one knows.

"Vertigo at Wolf Gap" originally appeared in *The Comstock Review.*

Funeral Arrangements
by Tim Rolands

I tell my wife I want a Viking funeral.
She says she's not about to throw herself
on any pyre, and I say no, not that part.
Just lay me out on a boat and light it up
out on the water under the open sky.

I don't want to go in a hole, buried in a box
to wither away into a bundle of dry meat
and bones dressed in my last good suit
like I'm on my way to an interview for yet another
job. By then I'll be retired well beyond résumés.

And I don't want to go to some industrial-grade
inferno on a factory floor churning out urns
full of ash for orders from around the world
and end up in a box in the attic or buried in the yard.

Boat on the water. Fiery blaze. Open sky. I say.
She says it's probably a violation of health code.

I look at her and see the irony, but she's serious, too.
In this state, I say, I'm sure it is.

So cremation, but send my ashes to space
in a silver canister to float at the edge of gravity
(with the rest of the junk),
and after decades or centuries,
when the orbit of my final reward decays,
I will plummet back down into the sky
riding through re-entry in my blazing capsule
like a phoenix flying out of the heavens!

The phoenix wasn't a Viking thing, she says.

Then call it a Valkyrie, I say.

My Father Returns from New York City
by Maureen Sherbondy

My father murmured in a hushed voice
(my ears overheard down the hall)
in an index finger over-the-lips shushed
kind of tone, *I hit a girl today,*

As if the wind had stirred up between city
buildings, propelling abandoned, disregarded
printed papers forward, damaged stories
flying across the streets and avenues.

He whispered to my mother, his voice
thick, tripping with liquor, *A bad girl,*
I hit a bad girl today with my car
(in a city lined with poverty, prostitutes).

These words—as if a small bird burst forth
from the nest, wings extended, and could not
fly. My father had once said to me
when the baby bird fell broken-winged

from the tree to the overgrown summer grass,
his lips so close to my face my cheek warmed,
We cannot save her. And I watched that
last breath push from her feathered chest.

If, in October
by Marilyn Taylor

If, in October
I should be driving past a row
of brick-and-shingle bungalows
when maple leaves are sticking to the sidewalk
and a rain-glossed school bus starts to swing
its yellow bulk around the corner,

there you are again—framed in a wavy
leaded window, watering a long-fingered
philodendron while the Victrola
clatters out Landowska's version of
the *Little Preludes* through the glass

and I am nine years old —and you,
the center of my small universe,
are the love of my life, to whose powdered
presence I come home blissfully,
day after dangerous day

utterly innocent of a distant time
when you will turn from me
and withdraw into my archive of losses.
Even your quaint name, *Alice,* melts
to nearly nothing on my tongue.

Stick Figure
by Rebecca Timson

After all these years I still can't attach
flesh to her bones, or face my father
who said it was my fault she left us:
I didn't love her enough, didn't see her
as she was or insist on her mothering.

But I was just his assistant. For him,
more than the one time, my mother
disappeared. Then he'd fetch her back
and make her vanish again, a one-trick
magician expertly performing sleight of fist.

After her last exit, in art class I drew her
as a stick figure without arms or head,
just a forked stick which could walk itself
to the river's edge and float away.

I've seen it and I know sticks can float
a long time—unless battered to bits,

say, by a rough descent through
rapids in a glacier-fed cataract—

floating where the river runs through
a flat land or whirls in the eddies
below wet boulders mid-stream.
(Did my mother know this, though her
stick-figure self had no head for knowing?)

Floating provides respite from wild waves
around the bend, but no matter: eventually
water enters every dead cell and drowns
the weighted branch. Or maybe one bit,

torn by the wind from a living tree,
is tossed ashore on a cliff-guarded beach
and takes new root in foreign soil:

Grows tall, blossoms, bears fruit.

Maybe it happened to my stick-mother. Maybe
some scrap of her escaped from the floating
and the battering, flowered outside the narrative
(like a monk's braided roses bordering the copied
text, not part of the manuscript but illuminating it)—

    free from any story I can conjure to give
    false substance to her weightless soul.

No Nice Guys

by Anne Vetter

The men aren't going to win shit here, and
why should they? On Thursday in the coffee shop
with the green walls, I hear about another *nice guy*
who got drunk, pushed his way through
a woman's body like she's the revolving door entrance
to a department store. All veins in me split-rip open
as soon as the story's out on the table, set between
the coffee and jam. This woman's words will be
worth about as much as dried rice, which is to say

not at all. See, I had a nice guy: he pulled music
from his guitar as nymphs pull flowers from bottoms of
lakes. Yet still, he grew fog in the space under his
skull when he set free his hands, unherded animals
over me. He tucked himself in like I was a bed,
linen duvet fluffed and turned over for his comfort,
his good night's rest. Sure, he was *sweet* about it. Sure he
kissed me the whole time like the inside of my mouth
was water-flowers, called me the morning after

to tell me I *cured him like spring cures the ground*
of snow, like salt-breeze carries the sea.
Shouldn't I've known *something* as soon as the skin
over me repelled itself from its muscle frame,
when I didn't touch myself for weeks? But, see,
even *I* didn't believe my body as much
as I believed that men like him, good men, men
tender like clovers under grass could use their fingers
like acid rain, like liver-rot, like all black dogs
with sharp teeth. I trusted myself about as much as
dandelion roots, which is to say, I didn't, not at all.

Love Letter for Floyd Patterson
by Jess Williard

It starts with my father curled on the floor
at the foot of his granddaughter's bed,

don't leave uttered for a second
then third time, enough not to shake

    the strange urgency of her three-year-old
    imperative,

this the third night my sister
hasn't shown up—

don't leave. He will sleep
but not dream, he will wake

    to a world that asks him to teach
    a language to people who could not possibly

wear it. The man has never been large.
And here, cradling dank air

so a three-year-old body, several feet away
and lax atop cotton bedding,

    may measure a kind of closeness
    in some other heat:

the man has never been large.
I do not need to mention the boxer,

all that humming, side-bending sinew,
unrelentingly tender even inside

    a ring, his curled body at the foot of anything,
    compactness, his compactness, his compactness—

I do not need to mention him silently
dismantling everything.

The man has never been large.
And any packaged history where two men

    circle each other with intentions
    is any packaged history where one

will stop to lay on the ground
to quell the other's loneliness. There is purpose

here. There is something to send
from a cower. It starts where it shouldn't

   and becomes mention of this world
   where to be small and furious is enough.

Bystander

by Jen Bergmark

The pond, manmade, felt real in a city with a concrete trench for a river. Shallow, green, bordered by wetland vegetation, a near-perfect circle about sixty feet across. Bass and bluegill drifted below the surface, introduced to the pond by Audubon volunteers and fished out later by neighborhood kids. When two figures approached on the trail, Nathan—resting, mid-hike, at the opposite bank with Sam, his border collie—thought *boys here to fish*. From his vantage point, partially blocked by papyrus reeds and cattails, he saw the boys didn't have fishing poles. Then he wasn't sure whether they were boys, or men. They wore Dodgers caps and walked with their heads down, hunched over, dragging their feet through the gravel, muttering to each other.

"Sit," Nathan whispered to Sam.

Earlier on his hike he'd passed a couple, the woman carrying a baby in a sling. Without them noticing, he aimed his Nikon. He passed a man walking a Labrador. On an uphill climb, he liked the charge he got when overtaking someone younger. Nathan was sixty-five years old and fit, with good posture and a full head of gray hair. The scar on his cheek had long ago worked itself into the lines of his face. He thought of it only when people noted its proximity to his eye and said "how lucky." Technically, you needed only one eye to take a photo, but you needed the other to see.

The figures approached the pond's edge. Their voices—he heard now, they were only boys—rose in volume, sounded urgent. They hadn't seen him shielding himself behind the reeds, holding his dog's collar. He'd meant to be home by now, grading student photographs before taking his wife to breakfast. Their routine, every Sunday. She would be waiting for him.

He moved aside a stalk of papyrus, and as he watched, one boy gave the other a rough jab to the shoulder. He lifted his camera. The boy shoved again and the other boy stumbled, nearly falling into the water. Then the boys began to fight, grappling, chest to chest, pulling, pushing away. A cap was knocked to the ground and trampled underfoot. Nathan clicked the shutter release, a thrumming behind his sternum like a shoplifter's thrill of getting away with it. These would be good photos. After breakfast he'd develop them in his darkroom. He used a 35mm camera, always. Digital was cheating.

Reflected tree branches darkened the pond. A breeze roughed the water's surface. In his viewfinder, the boys were becoming a blur. Something terrible was happening, and in the instant it took Nathan to understand, there it was. Sharp crack. Reverberation. A hawk burst from a pine. An animal skittered in the nearby brush. Nathan dropped his camera and the strap around his neck abruptly stopped its fall. It hit his stomach like a punch.

One of the boys lay on the ground. The other stood over him, holding a gun. For a moment there was a dazzling stillness. Then the boy on the ground began to twitch, opened his mouth and emitted a spume of blood. The standing boy slid the gun into the waistband of his jeans.

Nathan clamped his hand around the muzzle of his softly whining dog. He was trapped at the pond's edge. The trail head to his right was in plain view of the boy. Behind him stood a bank of trees and then a sandy ledge with a drop-off too steep to navigate. Somewhere out there was the couple with the baby in a sling, the man with the Labrador.

The boy with the gun stood stiffly, his arms hanging at his sides, blood approaching his sneakers. Nathan watched him scan the pond, his attention lingering at the spot where Nathan crouched. Seeing him? No, he was looking at the hazy skyscrapers of downtown Los Angeles in the distance, before he turned from the dead boy in the dirt and made his way down toward the picnic area.

*

When the boy disappeared from view, Nathan leapt up and headed the opposite way. He ran as fast as he could. His camera banged against his abdomen. His hiking boots struck the path with loud crunches, and under that sound he imagined he could hear the boy, behind him, advancing with light footfalls, two for his every one. The boy's hand would seize his shoulder. He'd feel the gun press against his back, hear the same echoing snap he'd just heard at the pond. A snap and then everything would go dark. He stumbled and dropped Sam's leash, but the dog kept pace, snout low to the ground, the leash dragging and kicking up dust. His cell phone was under the seat of his car where he'd forgotten it. The landscape bounced in his periphery, scrub and cactus. As he rounded a curve he lost his footing and slid painfully on his side while Sam jumped at him, roughly nosing his face.

Finally, half jogging, half limping, he reached the trail's end and the Audubon building—closed on Sundays. The dirt became pavement. His shoes smacked concrete. He found a graffiti-covered payphone at the edge of the parking lot and pulled the receiver from the cradle.

"Someone's been killed at Debs Park," he said.

Dead body by the pond. The emergency operator asked for his name. Nathan heard a rustling in the trees and dropped the phone and ran again, across the lot, where he hustled Sam into the back of his car and then fell into the driver's seat, chest heaving. He fumbled his keys into the ignition. His leg muscles quaked, his feet jittering on the floorboards. He managed, somehow, to drive, because he found himself on the road negotiating traffic, though he didn't remember getting there. It was just shy of nine o'clock, but already his car's interior broiled. Sweat rolled down his neck. He drove for several minutes before it occurred to him to crack a window for his dog, who panted dramatically in the back seat. At an intersection he looked at his camera in his lap and read the number in the frame counter.

*

Dead body. If you saw enough of them it shouldn't be a big deal. A photo in Nathan's most recent project, his *Skid*

Row series, was the image of a homeless man slumped beside a dumpster, rigor mortis canting his body at odd angles. He wore filthy trousers but brand new leather loafers, toes pointing skyward. Decades back, in Nathan's early photography days as a stringer for the A.P. in Vietnam, there were countless dead. Soldiers on stretchers. Whole families of corpses in piles. A severed leg alone in a field.

He was safe now. He was pretty sure he was safe. He kept checking the rearview mirror to look at the faces of drivers behind him. But none were the boy. Would he recognize the boy? What had so vividly played out for him moments before was a jumble. Nathan fanned through radio stations, searching, improbably, for some mention of it. He switched to AM. Nothing there either. The radio played traffic reports until he reached his driveway.

*

He expected Lydia to be waiting for him, but the fizzing sound of the shower met him as he entered their bedroom, Sam at his heels, still panting and alert to danger. Lydia had laid her day's outfit out on the bedspread—white cotton slacks, yellow linen blouse, sheer navy scarf. He put his camera on the dresser where she'd arranged the jewelry she chose for the day. He picked up her charm bracelet and fingered the charm for their daughter Liz, a ponytailed girl's head in profile, Liz's birth date engraved on the back. Liz was an adult now, married, living on the east coast. He put the bracelet down.

He headed to the half bathroom off the kitchen, dragging in a stool, stepping up so he could see his torso in the medicine cabinet mirror. He lifted his shirt and unbuckled his belt, wincing. The bruise on his hip was already purple.

Tomorrow his whole leg would be stiff. He splashed water on his face and ran a damp washcloth over his head and neck, tried to gather himself.

Back in the bedroom, he found the shower had stopped. He changed into a clean T-shirt and jeans, picked up his camera, wound the remaining unexposed negatives and then removed the film roll. He set it in the top drawer, amongst his socks.

Lydia emerged from the bathroom wrapped in a towel, her shoulders and chest damp and flushed.

"How was your hike?"

He'd reported it. But he hadn't identified himself to the operator. There had been a shooting last month outside the Arroyo Seco Library. Middle of the day, dozens of people saw it, and not one witness came forward. Things like this, you never knew. Could be a gang dispute, and there was a risk of retaliation. The important thing was he'd called. There were probably footprints near the body, or a bullet casing. The police would solve it.

"My hike was nice," he said.

*

On their walk to the restaurant, Lydia put her hand on his back, looked up at him, asked if he was limping.

"My knee is acting up," he said.

Their usual table on the sidewalk sat empty. Everyone else in their neighborhood was hunkered down in air conditioned rooms. Lydia, before taking her seat, gave him another look, one that reminded him, without insisting, to wear the knee support she'd bought him. Their friends called her *classy*, which had partly to do with clothing choices but more to do with her neutral approach to things.

She tolerated everyone's dramas and didn't burden anyone with her own.

"It's so hot," Lydia said to the waitress. "I'll have yogurt with fruit."

The table umbrella threw a feeble triangle of shade. The sunlight was a dense, metallic blaze. The air felt so parched and still that Nathan envisioned the boy beside the pond as a mummified husk, his blood a dry scrim, the pond stilled to murk. But it couldn't be so. EMTs would had driven an ambulance up the fire road. The boy must be gone, to the hospital, or the morgue. The day was pushing on as though nothing had happened.

Lydia spread a napkin across her lap, "I've been thinking about hanging wallpaper in the hall," she said. "I saw a pattern of birch trees."

Nathan wrestled apart the Sunday *Times*, looking for the local pages, which would say nothing about what he'd witnessed, but he felt compelled to look anyway.

Wallpaper. Over the years the hallway leading to their bedroom had become a repository for his photos, a narrow gallery. Sweat trickled along Nathan's torso. Would she hang his photos up again once wallpaper had been pasted to the wall, or did she mean to take them down? Why wallpaper, he wondered distractedly. Why now? There had been wallpaper all over their house when they moved there thirty years ago, huge flocked swaths of it. They were being modern, at the time, by taking it down.

Across the street, the hardware store door swung open and shut with customers. Lydia spooned yogurt into her mouth. Nathan spread out the arts section. It had nothing he wanted. He picked at his omelet while his iced coffee melted, hearing a faint wailing in the distance, a sound like cats fighting, which gradually grew louder, more insistent, until five police sedans screamed past. He jumped to his feet, rattling plates.

Lydia startled. "What's wrong?"

His heart was thudding. "I need salt," he said. He gestured to the waitress, who was also staring at him.

*

That evening he tried the TV news. A car under pursuit on the Pomona freeway and a theater in Westwood unfurling a red carpet. The weatherman predicted morning haze. But nothing about the boy. He tried his computer, realizing this should have been his first approach when a cursory search online pulled up an LAPD crime map. There was a menu of color-coded dots corresponding to recent crimes in Los Angeles. Orange for robbery. Blue for grand theft auto. Yellow for homicide. He moved the cursor until it hovered over Debs Park, and there it was, in the midst of the mottled topography, a small yellow bullet point.

Tipsters who wish to remain anonymous can call 'Crimestoppers,' said the LAPD website. He could do that. A quick phone call. Describe the boys and the gun and be done with it. He could crack open the film roll, expose the negatives to the sun, and toss the whole mess away.

He shut down his computer and went to the kitchen, where his wife had spread a pint of cherry tomatoes into soldierly rows on the cutting board. She was slicing each in half with a serrated knife.

Lydia had retired from social work the year before, a job where she navigated large-scale problems like spousal abuse and abandoned children. But she had stopped all talk of her former work, concentrating on small dilemmas—a slow sink drain, a broken floor tile, a skunk's nocturnal visit to her vegetable garden. And Nathan felt his own focus narrowing to the small details of her. Her slim reading glasses. Her narrow, teardrop-shaped fingernails. Her daily tasks played out in miniature. Rows of cherry tomatoes on the cutting board. Spare coins gathered in a jar. Recently she'd dug out a childhood stamp collection, and spent hours sifting though tiny paper squares that depicted flowers, fish, and royalty.

*

"There are photos you pursue and photos you receive," he said to his students.

He hadn't slept much. His head throbbed and there was a dull ache in his hip. A swell of exhaustion filled him as he looked over the faces in the lecture hall. The TA switched off the light. Nathan's photograph blinked onto the projection screen. He did this every term, mid-semester—his vanity show. There was a murmur of recognition. It was the photo everyone knew; it earned the big prize and launched his career.

Nathan looked at the familiar gradations of shadow. The photo was taken in daylight but under jungle canopy, so there was noise in the image, pinprick dots as though it had been printed on a sheet of sandpaper. The girl's eyes were two dark marbles.

The media had words for his photographs. *Unflinching. Uncompromising. Tough.*

Tough. He was twenty years old in Vietnam, skinny and cave-chested, with his camera hung like an unearned medal around his neck. Whenever something moved, he lifted the camera in trembling hands and pressed the release.

Later there was *"The Stalk,"* as he referred to it when interviewed: the calculating arrangement of people and things within the frame, the squeezing of shutter at ideal instant, the split second, opportunistic dance—but all that came later. In Vietnam he was a terrified kid.

"This is a photograph of receipt," he said. His students gazed above his head at the screen. "Call it luck or call it happenstance. But to receive you have to be open."

He'd been doing this so long it was rote; the image had become nothing more than an instructional tool for his students. But the pond and the gun and the blood. He looked up at the girl's face in the photo and saw, as if for the first time, the thin rim of white beyond her dilated pupils, her lips parted in the beginning of a scream. He had captured a mere shred of what must have felt, to her, like endless terror. Against his will, a fissure broke in his composure. He stopped talking.

The girl and her family had been swimming their escape across the river, their heads bobbing in the water, getting closer. At first his squad had aimed their rifles, but through squinted eyes the men saw two children and a woman. They waited. Nathan pulled off the lens cap. See something move, take out the camera. No shrapnel flying, no mangled bodies, but this war photo would win the award: the family fleeing the Viet Cong, struggling for shore, the daughter's terrified eyes caught in his lens just before she slipped underwater.

The squad rose from their crouched positions to see the woman and the boy scrabbling at the river bank, grasping for roots in the mud. Staff Sergeant Wayne Hall—newlywed, welterweight boxer from Munsee—stretched himself flat on the ground, leaning over the bank to pull them out. Lieutenant Richard Baker—lanky, Methodist, perpetually sunburnt—dove in after the girl with his helmet on.

The water came chest-high on Baker. The squad watched, transfixed, as Baker thrashed in the current, plunging under, surfacing with a gasp. Just when it seemed he'd give up, he dropped below and reemerged in a great splash with the sputtering girl. The squad shouted in relief. Nathan centered Baker in his viewfinder, got one last shot of him grinning and clasping her in a hug. On the riverbank the mother stood gripping her son's shoulders, staring ahead with a pained expression. Baker made a move toward shore. The girl in his arms looked to her mother and held up a grenade. The girl pulled the pin.

Nathan spent three weeks in a Medical Brigade Hospital—endotoxic shock, blood transfusions. He had a cloudy awareness that he was dying. Beyond his closed eyelids were the sounds of people working for his benefit: hurried footsteps, clank of metal, hiss of unraveling bandages. Then one day—Nathan had no idea how many days had passed—he was stable. With the fragment wounds on his chest taped and the torn-open side of his face closed with stitches, he was shipped home. Everyone else was dead, all ten in the squad, the mother, her son. The girl. Blown to bits. Somehow Nathan and his little Pentax had survived. The camera's body was battered, the viewfinder caked over with dried blood. The lens was smashed. But inside the film cavity, his negatives remained, curled safe within their cartridge, unharmed.

"Professor Zander?" The TA stood in the back of the room, hand on the light switch. The students sat very still. There were a few nervous coughs.

Nathan blinked and cleared his throat. How long had he been silent?

"To receive you have to be ready," he said. His voice was a rasp. The doomed girl towered over them all. "Okay," he said. His TA flipped the light switch.

*

Driving home from the university, he imagined himself telling Lydia. They would sit at the table, Sam dozing on the throw rug by the sink, outside the kitchen window the dark humps of the houses along the hill, beyond them a clutch of winking skyscrapers.

"I called 911," he would say. He imagined Lydia commiserating with him about the risks of retaliation, revisiting well-worn stories: the drive-by shooting near the freeway onramp, the school lockdown. They would talk about how these things usually happened just beyond their reach—the day after they drove through the intersection or the week they were away on vacation. But now it had hit home and they were part of it. Staring out the window, he'd know that Lydia wasn't really thinking about retaliation. She was thinking of a mother somewhere who'd lost her son. She was thinking about the right thing to do.

He could see them, standing side by side, staring out the dark window. He could see them both reflected in the glass. "You should go to the police," Lydia would say.

He pictured the drowning girl's frightened face printed beside whatever he'd captured in his Nikon at the pond. *Famous war photographer catches murder on film.* Two photographs of receipt, side by side.

Beside him, at the kitchen window, his elegant wife with her empathy stretching to the sea.

She would sigh. "Do the right thing," he imagined her saying softly. "This isn't about you."

But when he arrived, she was not at the kitchen table as he'd envisioned, but in the dining room, their old silverware arranged on the tablecloth before her along with a pile of sterling jewelry; she was polishing it all.

"Look at this," she said, holding out a tangle of bracelets when he entered the room. "Every one of these clasps is broken."

*

When their daughter was four years old, she'd asked about a cemetery they drove past. His wife was in the passenger seat, their daughter propped in the backward-facing folding bench in the rear of their station wagon. "A cemetery," Lydia said, and then she clumsily explained it.

"What happens after that?" their daughter asked.

He and Lydia exchanged looks.

"After that, you go to heaven," Lydia said, and in response to more questions she added that heaven was in the sky.

"How can I get there when my body is under the ground?" Liz asked. Nathan thought he heard a tearful edge to her voice.

"Well, your *body* doesn't go." Lydia was fiddling nervously with the latch of the glove compartment. "But *you* go."

There was a moment of silence in the back seat. "Can I see?" she said.

"What, honey?"

"In heaven. Can I see? Even with no body? Can I see everything?"

"Yes. You can see."

There was quiet again. Nathan thought her questions were satisfied when he heard Liz's soft sobs. He slowed the car and Lydia turned full around, kneeling on her seat. "Oh, honey," she said, reaching across the expanse of the station wagon. But their daughter was too far away. "What is it?"

"Am I eyes?" Liz cried. "Am I just eyes floating in the sky?"

"Of course not," Lydia said with a little laugh. But she couldn't explain and their daughter would not be consoled.

*

His photos: a teenager playing saxophone at Port Authority; tourists standing in the footprints at Grauman's; a baby asleep on a mat in a Somali hut.

Lydia, years ago, waiting alone on the sofa on a Sunday afternoon while he shut himself in his darkroom, stood in the safelight's glow as prints dripped on the line. Liz—now miles away with children of her own—riding her bicycle in the driveway. His family always at the edge. He felt deeply for them, but never followed them with his camera. He was searching elsewhere.

A student approached at the end of Thursday's class as Nathan gathered papers into his briefcase.

"These are late," the student said.

Nathan looked down at the folder the student had placed on his desk. "These were due last week."

"I know," he said. "I didn't do the film print you asked for. I was out finding the shots. These are all digital. You can knock points off my grade for that."

When Nathan didn't answer, the student looked at the floor. Nathan slid the prints from the folder. The first image was a color shot, soldiers in the back of an army jeep, probably heading up the 405 from Camp Pendleton. The vehicle looked enormous, cartoonish, with a sandy camouflage paint job. Beside the jeep was a strip of blurry freeway. The soldiers were smoking cigarettes, reaching down to tie boots, shrugging out of jackets in the late afternoon sun. One soldier had an expectant look, a yearning in his posture. He turned from the others, looking directly into the lens, his jaw thrust forward, about to say something. A message that the camera didn't catch.

"This is good," Nathan said.

"I hung out the passenger window of the car," the student said, eyes still downcast, smiling. "My girlfriend drove."

"You're good."

You're good. Or you're dead. It was something Lieutenant Baker used to say to the squad. It was supposed to be funny. Nathan remembered standing alone in the dark, newly home from the 27th Medical Brigade Hospital, waiting for his photo to emerge in the developing bath. White paper, gray shadow, and then the pricks of grain revealed. The fear in the girl's eyes. The river water, menacing, vast.

Like a sea monster should rise from it. *I'm alive*, Nathan had thought, feeling sick for thinking it.

"This is quality work," Nathan told the student. "This may save your grade, but don't let it go to your head."

*

Nathan steered through the gates of Deb's Park, Sam panting, eager for a hike, but there were still a half dozen speed bumps before they arrived at the parking lot. Each bump sent bile into Nathan's throat. He thought about turning back, but Sam whined as though sensing his thoughts. The park was filled with picnickers, even on a weekday. There were people cooking on grills, the music of an ice cream truck.

Nathan started up the fire road toward the pond and encountered three smiling women coming back down. The trail was sunny. There was a breeze. The Audubon volunteers had cleaned up the beer cans he noticed last time.

It was as though nothing criminal had occurred, and when Nathan reached the pond's edge, his memory was hazy. The film roll in the drawer would tell him. He stared at the water and imagined a coppery blood odor rising to his nostrils, but when he inhaled, he could smell only eucalyptus, maybe a hint of ozone. A man passing called out *beautiful day*.

*

He opened the dresser drawer where the film roll sat, inert and bland and identical to all other undeveloped rolls of film. Lydia, fully dressed, lay on the neatly made bed, reading a magazine. She was absorbed in an article and didn't look up.

In his darkroom he wound the negatives into the canister, added the fluid, shook it, set the timer. There was a familiar tang of stop-bath odor in his nostrils. Beyond the womb of his darkroom he could hear the clothes dryer tumbling. He waited. It seemed like forever, the waiting. So much of his life had been consumed by exactly this: waiting in the dark for an image he'd burned onto a coated slip of paper to speak to him, to tell him who he was, to convince him that he was more than just someone who watched, who took something away from people, by watching.

The timer rang. Nathan held the negatives to the light.

The couple with the baby in the sling. The hiker he'd passed on the trail. The Labrador sniffing the air. The trees swaying. The escalating argument. He didn't bother with a contact sheet or test strips. He positioned the negative he wanted into the enlarger.

Nathan watched the photo ripple into view in the developing bath. The boy falling into the moment of death. His torso and outstretched arms were reflected in the pond. It looked like there was someone, down below with the bass and bluegill, reaching up to receive him.

It was stunning. And he'd done nothing but flinch and press a button. The familiar swell within him, the charge; it was as good a photo as any he'd seen. He was still in the game.

Lydia was asleep when he returned to the bedroom, her reading glasses on, the magazine open on her chest. He gently pulled her glasses off and she waved an arm sleepily as if swatting a fly. He brushed her hair away from her face. Her haircut—a silver bob—was almost the same style she'd worn as a young woman, when her hair was light brown.

Back then she'd had severe bangs across her forehead, like a flapper in a Brassaï portrait. He had a photo of her from those days. He still remembered the aperture setting, the focus so tight on her eyes that the image went soft at her jaw line.

He lay down beside her. The mattress compressed only slightly under his weight. Lydia was miles away on her side of the bed. He felt no bigger than his dog. He lay on his back, his hands folded on his ribcage. People grew fatter in old age, he found himself thinking, because the alternative, skin against bone, was a reminder of where you were heading.

*

The following day wasn't a class day, but he drove to his office in the journalism department anyway, and sat as his desk. Below his window, students rushed across the green to their classes. He switched on his radio, found that the jazz station he liked was having a pledge drive, and switched it off again. After an hour, he had decided to leave when he heard a light tap on his door. He got up to answer it. It was the same student who'd approached him last class, with another late assignment.

"I was going to slide these under the door. Then I saw your light."

"I can fail you for not fulfilling the class requirements," Nathan said, but as he said it, he found himself eagerly returning to his desk to look at the photos. No contact sheet, again. The student hadn't used film, but Nathan could admit that he was tired of looking at film work of students who dutifully handed in gray contact sheets and muddy prints from negatives left in developing fluid too long.

The photos were colorful shots of elaborate graffiti and murals, and several lonely images of gang tags, and then Nathan came to images of a familiar landscape, a place he used to hike with Sam—the Glenoaks Canyon trail, burned by an arsonist months before. New growth was visible, anemic plant shoots pushing up through the char, but it was still otherworldly. The hillside was calcified. Skeletal trees had been scorched with a heat so intense that the blackened bark had split and peeled away, revealing heartwood that was surprisingly, vividly red. Someone had carved their initials into a tree's bright center.

The student stood beside Nathan's chair, fidgeting with the zipper of his jacket. "This series is called, *Everyone Needs to Make their Mark*," he said.

Nathan collected the photos into the folder.

"It's actually my girlfriend's title. She came up with it."

"Is your girlfriend a photographer too?" Nathan asked. He noticed the student smile slightly at being called a photographer.

"She's not," he said. "She likes to help me."

"I'll take quality into consideration when determining your grade." Nathan turned back to the book open on his desk. "You could try film," he said as the student was leaving. "Try out the darkroom. Just to see what it's like."

*

The finished print was eight-by-ten, glossy. He turned it over on his darkroom work table and autographed the back in wax pencil, by habit, as he'd done for years. Then he neatly printed the date, location, his name and contact information, slid it into a cardboard mailer and affixed a label addressed to the Hollenbeck Division homicide detectives.

He put Sam into the back of his car and drove to the post office.

The following morning he and Sam took a long hike, in Angeles National Forest. There were streams that rushed over rock ledges, forming cold, clear pools. There were rotting branches teeming with ladybugs. Sam jumped and crashed through leaves, barking. Nathan watched it all through the viewfinder. Lydia, back at home, would be taking his photos down from the walls, carefully wrapping them in bubble wrap for storage before she ordered wallpaper from a catalog.

Eastbound Train

by Andrea Hansell

The two girls sat together on the frozen ground, their backs against the rough wooden fence that ran along the side of the railway platform. Their wool cloaks were pulled over their heads to block both wind and unwelcome attention. Golda's arm had grown numb from the weight of her younger sister's head on her shoulder. She tried to shift position gently, imperceptibly, but Milka stirred and woke. "Has a train come yet?" she asked.

"Two pulled in while you were sleeping," Golda said. "Freight trains with no passenger cars. Soldiers loaded them up with boxes."

"Boxes of what?" Milka asked.

"Rifles and grenades," Golda said. She didn't actually know what was in the boxes. It seemed important today, though, that Milka think she knew the answers to all questions.

"I'm hungry," Milka said.

Milka was always hungry these days. Already she was taller than Golda, her body curving into a softness that made men's eyes linger—their brother-in-law Tuvya's eyes, and, more worrisome, the vodka-fueled eyes of the Russian soldiers who roamed the snow-packed streets of Berdichev like packs of stray dogs. One afternoon last week some soldiers had taken two Jewish girls, friends of Milka's, to their camp on the edge of town. The girls, pale and shivering, walked home hours later through the silent dark. The girls' mother told Golda's older sister Raisel that the soldiers had made them peel potatoes. Raisel's pursed lips suggested she did not believe only potato skins had been removed. Golda knew the soldiers were unlikely to look at her own pock-marked face and flat chest. But young, blooming Milka was at risk. The well-being of girls was valued little in Berdichev, and the lives of Jewish girls mattered not at all.

"I'm hungry," Milka said again. "We should have brought more bread."

"We'll eat when we get home," Golda said. "Mama will make soup and cake for us."

The wind blew dark clouds over the pale afternoon sun, throwing blue shadows over the fields of wheat stubble beyond the train tracks. Those fields had been green when Golda and Milka arrived last June, a summer scented breeze carrying bird song and bee hum to the passengers stepping down from the sweltering train cars. They had been sent to help Raisel with her new twin babies—a summer adventure in Berdichev. They were to return home in the fall to resume their studies, Milka in the village school and Golda at the Jewish girls' high school in Kiev.

For several weeks they had delighted in the luxuries of Raisel and Tuvya's big house. Though they spent tedious hours rocking infants, sweeping the kitchen floor, and chopping vegetables, their reward was a big feather bed and meals with plenty of meat. Sometimes they were allowed to accompany Tuvya when he went to buy the fur pelts that he stitched into warm coats and blankets for the city's wealthiest citizens. At the bustling Berdichev Fair they inhaled the scent of exotic spices, watched the acrobats and jugglers perform for the crowds, and listened to the strolling balalaika players whose soft music intertwined with the raucous cries of merchants hawking their goods. After a day at the fair, Golda would lie in the soft bed next to Milka dreading the end of summer and the return to their small, sleepy village.

Then an Austrian duke was assassinated and a war broke out. The girls spent the first chilly days of autumn crouched in Raisel's damp, earth-smelling root cellar, rocking the ever-fretful babies as the thud and bang of nearby battles assaulted their ears. By the time the Russian forces drove the Austro-Hungarians westward into Galicia and quiet returned to Berdichev, the trains had stopped carrying civilian passengers. Only soldiers, medical personnel and munitions shipments passed through the half-empty stations. Even the mail was no longer sent eastward on the trains. It had been months since they'd heard from their parents, or, Golda supposed, since their parents had heard from them. She didn't like to think how worried her mother must be about her two youngest daughters. She herself often worried late into the night, as the wind howled and soldiers sang drunkenly on the muddy street outside her window. While Milka breathed deeply and evenly beside her under the thick goose down quilt, Golda would turn restlessly onto her back, then back to her side again, her mind churning like mud under wagon wheels. Were her parents safe, the little house standing, her father still loading his tools into the wagon at dawn as the old mule brayed by the rundown fence?

Milka's voice brought Golda back to the windy train platform. "It's getting late," Milka said. "When we're not back for dinner, Raisel will send Tuvya looking for us."

"If the next train isn't a passenger train, we'll walk back to Raisel's house," Golda said. "We'll be punished, but it's better than freezing to death."

"And if the next train *is* a passenger train? How will we get on?"

"Don't worry," Golda assured her. "I have a plan."

But her plan was hazy. The first steps had been well thought out. After she'd decided to take Milka home to their parents, Golda had waited for an opportunity to leave Raisel's house unescorted. This morning when Raisel asked them to take a fur blanket over to her friend Rivka's for the new baby, Golda had realized that this was their chance. The sequence of events she had concocted during those sleepless, tossing nights must happen now, today: Layer three dresses one on top of the other because they couldn't be seen carrying luggage. Tuck bread into their cloaks. Tell Raisel they would stay at Rivka's for a while to visit. Write a note for Rivka's husband to bring to Raisel tomorrow so she wouldn't worry that they'd been taken by wolves or soldiers. Drop off the baby blanket and the note, then walk the long, cold miles to the train station. This was as far as the plan had extended.

Now it was Golda who drifted to sleep, leaning against her sister. Milka woke her from a confused dream in which soldiers led her father's mule through the streets of Berdichev with ominous black ribbons tied in his mane, and women called down to them from the roofs of houses. Waking, she still heard the voices of the dream women and realized that real women were talking loudly on the railway platform.

Golda peered through the deepening twilight at the cluster of women. There were nine of them, wearing the grey capes and white head coverings of army nurses. They spoke in Russian, their laughter warming the frigid wind that stung Golda's cheeks.

"Good-bye to Berdichev and the evil chief of surgery!"

"Are they sending you to the hospital in Kremenchuk, too?"

"Yes. I hope the wounded soldiers smell better there."

Kremenchuk. Their uncle lived there, less than an hour's sleigh ride from their own village.

"Stand up," Golda said, pulling the cloak back from Milka's face. She wound her sister's long braids around her head and secured them with one of her own hairpins. Milka's hair was silky, so different from Golda's own broom straw hair.

"Ouch," Milka said, squirming away from her. "What are you doing?"

"Making you look older," Golda said. "We're going to pretend we're nurses. They're going to Kremenchuk, where Uncle Ephraim lives."

"We don't look old enough to be grown-ups," Milka said. "Even *you* don't. And we don't have capes."

"That's because…" Golda closed her eyes and concentrated. "We're nursing students. We haven't earned our capes yet."

"Jewish girls aren't permitted in nursing schools," Milka said.

"Who says we're Jewish?" Golda said, switching from Yiddish to Russian. "I'm Olga, and you're Katya, two nice Russian girls."

"It won't work," Milka said, making a bleating noise like a frightened goat. Several of the nurses turned their heads towards the sound.

"Stop it!" Golda hissed. She tugged her sister into the shadows and grabbed her by the shoulders. Her mother would never shake Milka so roughly. She might shake Golda, but not pretty little Milka.

"They're looking at us," Golda told Milka. "Don't you want to go home?"

Her throat closed and stuck on the word "home." She had focused so intently on getting Milka there, on bringing her back to the warmth and safety of their parents' house. But now, she, Golda, was cold and scared and lonely and wanted to nuzzle her face into her mother's apron like the mule did when he wanted a carrot.

Milka continued to whimper.

"Can we help you?" one of the nurses called, a tall woman with sharp cheekbones and deep set eyes.

"We're fine," Golda said, speaking her best Russian and holding her back straight to look taller. "My friend just said good-bye to her sweetheart in Berdichev. Do you know when the train is supposed to come? We're heading to a nursing school in Kremenchuk to prepare for war duty."

They heard it then, the clackety-clack of wheels, the screech of brakes.

"Well, I guess you summoned the train," the tall nurse said. "Get on with us. We're going to Kremenchuk too."

The women clustered around the train, calling to each other in high-pitched voices, and Golda shepherded Milka into the group. The door of one of the train cars clanked open, and a stern conductor unfolded a metal ladder. "Climb up," Golda whispered. "We're going to Kremenchuk."

The two girls climbed the ladder and followed the nurses into a dark, narrow corridor. The conductor led them past several wooden compartments full of official looking people in uniforms, then slid open the door to an empty compartment at the furthest end of the car. The narrow space contained two long benches which faced each other. As the nurses stopped to hoist their belongings onto the luggage racks above the benches, Golda tugged Milka past them so they could sit at the end of the forward facing bench, next to the scratched and dirty window.

"Who are these two?" asked one of the nurses, removing her white head covering and shaking out a mass of wild red hair. "These benches will be crowded enough with just the nine of us."

"They're nursing students," said the tall woman who had spoken to them outside the train. "And luckily they're young enough to have skinny behinds."

A small blonde nurse giggled. "You wouldn't have to worry so much about crowded benches if you didn't like potatoes so much," she told the redhead.

The three friends seated themselves by the window on the bench facing Golda and Milka, and the other nurses found seats further along the two benches.

"Tell us your names, nursing students," said the tall woman. "We have a long ride together. We may as well get acquainted."

"I'm Olga," Golda said. "And this is my friend Katya."

The tall nurse looked at them for a moment, long enough for Golda to wonder if she accepted the false names. Then she smiled at them. The smile looked warm and genuine, crinkling her eyes and making them look less like those of a bird of prey. "I'm Oksana," she said.

The tiny nurse with the yellow hair introduced herself as Natalya. The redhead was Maruska. Golda recited the names to herself so she would remember them. Then she rehearsed their own new names. She must answer to Olga for the rest of this trip, and make sure Milka remembered to be Katya.

The train sat at the station for a long time. The nurses chattered among themselves, and Golda was relieved that they did not ask her any more questions. As the night pressed black and impenetrable against the train window, the interior of the compartment darkened and the nurses' voices dwindled to breathy whispers.

"Why isn't the train moving?" Milka said.

Golda was relieved to hear her speak Russian. "Be patient, Katya," she replied, but she thought, *we'll never leave Berdichev. Tuvya will come and find us here and our plan will fall apart.*

Tuvya didn't come, though, and the train started. A hiss of steam, a loud whistle, then the car began to sway as the wheels rattled across the worn tracks. After a few minutes Golda heard rustling sounds and smelled food. Her stomach rumbled, her mouth filling with saliva. Someone lit a candle, casting a flickering yellow light across the compartment, and Golda saw that the nurses were pulling food out of their rucksacks.

"I'm hungry," Milka said in Yiddish.

"Be hungry in Russian," Golda whispered.

Oksana's dark eyes gleamed in the candlelight as she looked at the two girls. "Didn't you young ladies bring food?" she asked.

Golda shook her head. "Our luggage was stolen," she said.

"Poor lambs," said Oksana.

She spoke to her two friends. "Natalya! Maruska! We have food enough to share with our hungry nursing students, don't we?"

Golda and Milka watched as Oksana cut into a round, dark loaf with an army knife she had pulled from the folds of her cloak. Her friends busied themselves cutting slices from large hunks of grey meat and waxy yellow cheese. They handed these slices to Oksana, who layered them onto the dense brown bread.

Milka's eyes widened. "Meat and cheese," she whispered to Golda, again in Yiddish. Meat and dairy were never served together at Jewish tables. *Don't cook a goat in its mother's milk*, the Torah instructed them.

"What did you say, Katya?" Oksana asked Milka.

Golda kicked at Milka's leg, hard.

"I said that smells good," Milka said in Russian.

Oksana stood up, swaying with the motion of the train, and handed two sandwiches across to them. Golda looked down at the forbidden food and up into Milka's questioning eyes. She remembered her father telling her, when they had broken the Sabbath to take her dying baby brother to the doctor in the mule cart, that Jewish laws could be violated in order to preserve life. What would happen to them if the nurses learned that they weren't Olga and Katya, two ordinary Russian nursing students familiar with this food? Their lives would be in danger, wouldn't they?

Closing her eyes, Golda took a tiny, trial nibble of her sandwich. The fatty, unkoshered meat tasted metallic, and the cheese was strong and sour. For a moment she felt unable to swallow and worried she would choke. But she was hungry, very hungry, and they were being watched. She swallowed, then took a bigger bite.

"Eat!" she whispered to Milka, and Milka ate.

Natalya reached across from the opposite bench and handed them a metal canteen. "Have some water to wash your food down, girls," she said.

"Wait," said Maruska. "I have something better than water."

She pulled a silver flask from her large bosom, uncapped it, and drank deeply. They could see her cheeks flush even in the dim candlelight. She passed the bottle to Golda. Golda took a small sip, feeling the burn of alcohol as it slid down her throat. Her eyes watered and she coughed.

"You remind me of my sister," Oksana said. "She tried so hard to seem grown up, but she could never swallow brandy without coughing."

Maruska took the flask from Golda and offered it to Milka. "Katya?" she asked.

Milka shook her head.

Golda rolled her eyes. "Such a goody goody," she said.

"She can't be as proper as all that," Oksana said. "Didn't you tell us she had a boyfriend in Berdichev?"

"Oh, yes," Golda said. "Ivan. A real charmer."

"Ooh, tell us about him," Maruska said. "What does he look like, Katya?"

Milka shifted in her seat next to Golda. "Wavy blonde hair," she said. "Blue eyes."

"Is he a good kisser?" Natalya asked.

"I guess so," Milka said. "He … he was my first."

"I'm sure they did more than kiss," Maruska said. "Cold winter nights in Berdichev bring out the fire in young lovers."

"Yes," Oksana said, "And such fires can burn young women."

"Where's your sense of romance, Oksana?" Natalya said. "Young women aren't as silly as you think."

The compartment grew quiet. Golda lay back against the hard wooden seat and thought about kissing Milka's imaginary suitor. The train rocked her gently, as Ivan held her in his arms. She slept.

Early in the morning the train jolted to a stop at a country station. Golda saw the sun peeking over a snowy horizon, outlining the dark shapes of cattle huddled together in a barren field. The conductor yanked open the door to their compartment, sending a blast of frigid air into the stale interior which still smelled of last night's meat and cheese.

"You can get out here," he said. "Fifteen minutes. Go to the far side of the train if you want privacy."

"Yes, yes," Oksana said. "We've done this before. We're train stop veterans."

"Should we go?" Milka whispered to Golda. "I have to … you know."

Golda considered. Would they check papers when people got back on the train? They hadn't checked papers in Berdichev, and she, too, had an urgent need to relieve herself. She couldn't face sitting for a whole day in three layers of cold, soaked dresses.

"Hey come on, baby nursing students," Maruska called to them, tucking her red curls under her white nurse's scarf. "The toilet is over there next to the cows!"

Golda and Milka followed the grey-caped nurses out to the field. Like a row of perching birds, the nurses squatted and lifted their skirts, leaving steaming patches of yellow on the ice-crusted snow. Hoisting up their own multiple layers of dresses was a challenge, but the girls felt relieved when they had finished. They imitated the nurses, who were rubbing snow between their hands and using the melted slush to wash their faces. With her hair up and her cheeks pink from the snow bath, Milka looked beautiful. Milka would meet her Ivan someday, Golda thought. *If we ever make it home.*

Back on the train the nurses talked and laughed.

"I wish we had coffee," said a nurse at the far end of the bench.

"Remember that coffee at the Berdichev fair?" Maruska said. "The good, strong stuff the old Jew sold?"

"I never dared to taste it," Natalya said. "What if he'd poisoned it?"

"Why would he do that?" Oksana asked. "Poisoning customers seems like a quick way to lose a business."

"Why do Jews do any of the terrible things they do?" said Natalya.

"I've heard they kill Christian babies so they can drink their blood at the Passover meal," said the nurse who sat next to Golda.

"If you ask me," said a nurse further down the bench, "Catherine the Great should have given them all back to Poland when she had the chance."

Golda felt Milka's hand creep into hers.

"Let's hope that the Czar keeps them under good control," said Maruska. "I really did love the old Jew's coffee."

Oksana looked towards Golda and Milka, her face hard and angular in the bright morning light. Golda dropped Milka's hand. "Olga," Oksana said. 'Tell us about your nursing school in Kremenchuk. What is the course of study like?"

"It's a special course in war medicine," Golda said. "How to help with bullet wounds and amputations." She was amazed by how quickly the lies came to her lips. She worried, though, were the nurses familiar with the Kremenchuk nursing program? Had any of them studied there, or taught there?

The nurses' expressions remained genial and interested. "War medicine isn't just about battle injuries," Natalya said. "There's measles, and the flux, and syphilis to deal with too."

"Oh, they teach that as well," Golda said. She could almost see the nursing school now, the polished floors and the worn wooden study tables, the labeled color pictures of bones and organs.

"What was the nursing school like in St. Petersburg, Maruska?" Oksana asked, and the conversation moved safely away from Golda and Milka.

In the afternoon they stopped at another station. Pine-forested hills rose up in the distance. A ragged looking army band waited at the station for a train, but not their train. Maruska laughed and flirted with the trumpet player, and when the conductor summoned the women back to their car, the band serenaded them with a march. The train pulled away and headed eastward again, the cheerful, brassy music fading into the distance.

"I would have liked more time with that trumpet player," Maruska said to Milka. "I bet he kisses like your Ivan."

"Come get some air in the aisle with me, Olga," Oksana said, wrapping her long fingers around Golda's wrist. "Let Katya stay here with Maruska. The silly geese can talk about handsome soldiers to their hearts' content."

She wants to talk to me in private, Golda thought, feeling her heart quicken. *About what?* She gave Milka a look that said, *stay focused,* and followed Oksana out into the long, narrow corridor that ran alongside the train compartments. They leaned against the smooth outer wall of their compartment to brace themselves against the train's movement, and faced the windows that ran along the corridor.

"I worry about those lovesick girls," Oksana said, lighting a cigarette. "They'll learn soon enough that their fairy tale princes turn to drunken pigs at the stroke of midnight. I'd advise you to watch your young friend."

"Oh, I do," Golda said, and this, at least, wasn't a lie.

"Don't tell on me for smoking," Oksana said. "Now tell me where you came from, and about your family."

As Golda wove her story—a childhood in Berdichev, her father a postal clerk—the afternoon sun slanted golden through the bare trees lining the railway tracks, and glittering sunbeams hovered in the swirling dust of the train car. From time to time she tried to catch a glimpse into the compartment behind her to see how Milka was handling herself. Eventually she noticed that Oksana looked dreamy and didn't seem to be listening. Uncertain, she broke off in mid-sentence.

Registering the silence, Oksana looked up. "Forgive me, Olga," she said. "I was thinking of Lilya. You remind me of her a bit."

"Who is Lilya?" Golda asked. She hoped Lilya wasn't Jewish.

"Lilya was my sister," Oksana said. "Do you have a sister?"

"No," Golda said. "Just brothers. The oldest is in the army. The youngest, Misha, is still in school. And oh, he's full of mischief! He always misbehaves in church."

Again she almost believed her own story. She pictured her imaginary big brother, broad-shouldered in his uniform, and the playful Misha who held the spirit of her real brother, the baby who had died of pneumonia.

When Oksana finished her cigarette, they returned to the compartment. Golda entered to hear Milka laughing loudly with Maruska and Natalya. Golda slid in beside her next to the window. When the train passed through a noisy tunnel, Milka whispered in her ear. "I told good lies," she said. "It was fun, like making up stories about dolls. They like us, I think."

"They like Olga and Katya," Golda whispered back. "They might not like *us*."

In the middle of the night the train screeched to a stop and jerked them awake. Golda wiped at the foggy, grime-smeared window, and peered out. She saw nothing, just the gray-white banks of snow along the tracks and, when she craned her neck to look up, a crescent moon in a frozen black sky. The nurses murmured around them.

"What's the problem?"

"Is there a cow on the tracks?"

The outer door to the train car creaked open, and they heard rough male voices. A compartment door was opened, and there was muffled talking, questions and answers. Oksana put her finger to her lips and Golda held her breath, listening with all the others for the story of what was happening. Another compartment door opened, one closer to theirs. The nurses stirred, fastening capes and hiding their disheveled hair under the white head covers.

Soon their own compartment door opened, and lantern light lit up the faces of the women sitting on the benches and the red, stubbled face of the soldier holding the lantern. "Well, look at this!" he said. "Our noble ladies of the battle-field enema."

"Papers!" said another soldier, moving in front of the lantern to enter the compartment. "Get out your papers, please, ladies."

The nurses fumbled with their rucksacks, and Golda heard the crinkling of paper.

"Do you have our papers, Golda?" Milka whispered.

"Shhh," Golda said. "Pretend you're asleep." She pulled her cloak over both their heads and leaned into the cold surface of the train window.

"Oh, nurse!" said the soldier with the lantern. "I think I have the clap. Can you examine me?"

"Keep your hands to yourself!" they heard Maruska exclaim.

"Show some respect, soldier," Oksana said. "We're heading to the surgical hospital in Kremenchuk to treat your wounded brothers."

Golda felt the cloak being tugged from over her head, and saw light reflecting off a row of gold buttons. The soldier who leaned over her smelled of vodka and onions.

"Wake up, ladies!" he said. "I need to see your papers."

Fear froze Golda's tongue to the roof of her mouth. She felt Milka trembling beside her.

The other soldier moved the lantern so it shown into Golda's eyes. "That one looks like a toad," he said.

The pool of lantern light moved and came to rest on Milka. "Now that one," he said, "Is a pearl. I like diving for pearls, especially when they have no papers. Bring her here."

The soldier inside the compartment pulled Milka up by the shoulder. He turned her wrist and began to stroke the soft skin on the underside of her wrist, slowly, rhythmically. Milka drew a sharp breath.

"Hey!" called the lantern holder. "I said that one was mine. You can have the toad."

"I don't want the toad," the other soldier said. He tried to push Milka in the direction of the doorway, but she was frozen, unable to move her feet. The soldier struck her in the back, and she let out a cry, but still didn't move. The lantern holder stepped into the compartment and pulled on her arm, dragging her across the floor. The other soldier pushed her out of the compartment into the corridor behind them.

Maybe they'll just take her, Golda thought. *And I'll get home and eat Mama's cake.* Immediately she hated herself for thinking that. It was her job to protect Milka. She would die for her if she had to. She strained to see her sister in the dark corridor behind the soldiers. She saw that one of Milka's braids had fallen out of its pin, making her look even younger.

Oksana stood up. She was taller than the soldiers. "These girls are traveling with us," she said. "Their luggage and papers never arrived at the station. Stolen, probably. You know what Berdichev is like these days."

"Oksana," Natalya started to say, but Maruska hushed her.

"They'll need to come off the train with us," said the soldier who held Milka's arm. "This one and the toad."

"Really?" said Oksana. "In the middle of the night? The hospital chief will be angry when we arrive without them. Will you stop them from serving their czar and their country because of some stolen luggage?"

"I wonder," said the soldier with the lantern, looking at Oksana, "What the penalty is for hiding illegal travelers during wartime?"

Golda heard whispering among the nurses.

The soldier holding Milka drew her closer to him and she made her bleating goat noise.

"Leave her alone," Oksana said. She was trying to stay calm, but her voice quavered slightly. "We'll make an official complaint. We know who you are."

The soldier with the lantern looked out the window towards the moon, considering. "Let her go," he said to his companion.

"Are you sure?" asked Milka's captor. "It's a pity to lose this beauty."

The lantern holder turned the light on Milka, reached out his free hand, and traced the line of her full lower lip. "Agreed," he said. "But there will be others without mother hens protecting them."

He swung the lantern again so it shone into Golda's eyes. "Get your papers in order as soon as you get to Kremenchuk," he said.

The soldiers shoved Milka back into the compartment and shut the door with a bang, leaving the women in darkness. Golda heard Milka sobbing quietly, and the reassuring murmurs as kind hands passed her along to her spot next to Golda by the window. The train lurched forward, stopped, then started again. As it picked up speed, Oksana stood up unsteadily and put her hands on Golda's shoulders.

"Breathe," she said. "They're gone. Your Katya is safe."

Golda felt the tears come then, and she leaned her head forward and burrowed into Oksana's bony chest. She cried noisily, cried as she hadn't allowed herself to cry since the first autumn battles had trapped them in Berdichev. As she snorted and hiccupped, she felt Oksana stroke her hair. "Thank you," Golda said.

Oksana patted her arm and turned to sit down on her own bench. "By the way, Olga," she said. "You should know there is no nursing school in Kremenchuk."

Golda tried to make out Oksana's expression across from her in the darkness. *Lilya was my sister,* she thought. *Was.*

She wiped her tears on her sleeve and put her arm around Milka. The train rocked them back and forth, rocked them like Raisel's babies in their small wooden cradle. She hummed a fragment of a Yiddish lullaby her mother used to sing to her. If the train made good time and Uncle Ephraim's horses were sufficiently rested, perhaps they would be home in time for supper.

Glossolalia

by David Jauss

That winter, like every winter before it, my father woke early each day and turned up the thermostat so the house would be warm by the time my mother and I got out of bed. Sometimes I'd hear the furnace kick in and the shower come on down the hall and I'd wake just long enough to be angry that he'd woken me. But usually I slept until my mother had finished making our breakfast. By then, my father was already at Goodyear, opening the service bay for the customers who had to drop their cars off before going to work themselves. Sitting in the sunny kitchen, warmed by the heat from the register and the smell of my mother's coffee, I never thought about him dressing in the cold dark or shoveling out the driveway by porch light. If I thought of him at all, it was only to feel glad he was not there. In those days my father and I fought a lot, though probably not much more than most fathers and sons. I was sixteen then, a tough age. And he was forty, an age I've since learned is even tougher.

But that winter I was too concerned with my own problems to think about my father's. I was a skinny, unathletic, sorrowful boy who had few friends, and I was in love with Molly Rasmussen, one of the prettiest girls in Glencoe and the daughter of a man who had stopped my father on Main Street that fall, cursed him, and threatened to break his face. My father had bought a used Ford Galaxie from Mr. Rasmussen's lot, but he hadn't been able to make the payments and eventually Mr. Rasmussen repossessed it. Without a second car my mother couldn't get to her job at the school lunchroom, so we drove our aging Chevy to Minneapolis, where no one knew my father, and bought a rust-pitted yellow Studebaker. A few days later Molly Rasmussen passed me in the hall at school and said, "I see you've got a new car," then laughed. I was so mortified I hurried into a restroom, locked myself in a stall, and stood there for several minutes, breathing hard. Even after the bell rang for the next class, I didn't move. I was furious at my father. I blamed him for the fact that Molly despised me, just as I had for some time blamed him for everything else that was wrong with my life—my gawky looks, my discount store clothes, my lack of friends.

That night, and others like it, I lay in bed and imagined who I'd be if my mother had married someone handsome and popular like Dick Moore, the PE teacher, or Smiley Swenson, who drove stock cars at the county fair, or even Mr. Rasmussen. Years before, my mother had told me how she met my father. A girl who worked with her at Woolworth's had asked her if she wanted to go out with a friend of her boyfriend's, an army man just back from the war. My mother had never agreed to a blind date before, or dated an older man, but for some reason this time she said yes. Lying there, I thought about that fateful moment. It seemed so fragile—she could as easily have said no and changed every-thing—and I wished, then, that she had said no, I wished she'd said she didn't date strangers or she already had a date or she was going out of town—anything to alter the chance conjunction that would eventually produce me.

I know now that there was something suicidal about my desire to undo my parentage, but then I knew only that I wanted to be someone else. And I blamed my father for that wish. If I'd had a different father, I reasoned, I would be better looking, happier, more popular. When I looked in the mirror and saw my father's thin face, his rust-red hair, downturned mouth, and bulging Adam's apple, I didn't know who I hated more, him or me. That winter I began parting my hair on the right instead of the left, as my father did, and whenever the house was empty I worked on changing my voice, practicing the inflections and accents of my classmates' fathers as if they were clues to a new life. I did not think, then, that my father knew how I felt about him, but now that I have a son of my own, a son almost as old as I was then, I know different.

If I had known what my father was going through that winter, maybe I wouldn't have treated him so badly. But I didn't know anything until the January morning of his breakdown. I woke that morning to the sound of voices downstairs in the kitchen. At first I thought the sound was the wind rasping in the bare branches of the cottonwood outside my window, then I thought it was the radio. But after I lay there a moment I recognized my parents' voices. I couldn't tell what they were saying, but I knew they were arguing. They'd been arguing more than usual lately, and I hated it—not so much because I wanted them to be happy, though I did, but because I knew they'd take their anger out on me, snapping at me, telling me to chew with my mouth closed, asking me who gave me permission to put my feet up on the coffee table, ordering me to clean my room. I buried one ear in my pillow and covered the other with my blankets, but I could still hear them. They sounded distant, yet somehow close, like the sea crashing in a shell held to the ear. But after a while I couldn't hear even the muffled sound of their voices, and I sat up in the bars of gray light slanting through the blinds and listened to the quiet. I didn't know what was worse: their arguments or their silences. I sat there, barely breathing, waiting for some noise.

Finally I heard the back door bang shut and, a moment later, the Chevy cough to life. Only then did I dare get out of bed. Crossing to the window, I raised one slat of the blinds with a finger and saw, in the dim light, the driveway drifted shut with snow. Then my father came out of the garage and began shoveling, scooping the snow furiously and flinging it over his shoulder, as if each shovelful were a continuation of the argument. I couldn't see his face, but I knew that it was red and that he was probably cursing under his breath. As he shoveled, the wind scuffed the drifts around him, swirling the snow into his eyes, but he didn't stop or set his back to the wind. He just kept shoveling fiercely, and suddenly it occurred to me that he might have a heart attack, just as my friend Rob's father had the winter before. For an instant I saw him slump over his shovel, then collapse face-first into the snow. As soon as this thought came to me, I did my best to convince myself that it arose from love and terror, but even then I knew part of me wished his death, and that knowledge went through me like a chill.

I lowered the slat on the blinds and got back into bed. The house was quiet but not peaceful. I knew that somewhere in the silence my mother was crying and I thought about going to comfort her, but I didn't. After a while I heard my father rev the engine and back the Chevy down the driveway. Still I didn't get up. And when my mother finally came to tell me it was time to get ready, her eyes and nose red and puffy, I told her I wasn't feeling well and wanted to stay home. Normally she would have felt my forehead and cross-examined me about my symptoms, but that day I knew she'd be too upset to bother. "Okay, Danny," she said. "Call me if you think you need to see a doctor." And that was it. She shut the door and a few minutes later I heard the whine of the Studebaker's cold engine, and then she was gone.

It wasn't long after my mother left that my father came home. I was lying on the couch in the living room watching TV when I heard a car pull into the driveway. At first I thought my mother had changed her mind and come back to take me to school. But then the back door sprang open and I heard him. It was a sound I had never heard before, and since have heard only in my dreams, a sound that will make me sit up in the thick dark, my eyes open to nothing and my breath panting. I don't know how to explain it, other than to say that it was a kind of crazy language, like speaking in tongues. It sounded as if he were crying and talking at the same time, and in some strange way his words had become half-sobs and his sobs something more than words—or words turned inside out, so that only their emotion and not their meaning came through. It scared me. I knew something terrible had happened, and I didn't know what to do. I wanted to go to him and ask what was wrong, but I didn't dare. I switched off the sound on the TV so he wouldn't know I was home and sat there staring at the actors mouthing their lines. But then I couldn't stand it anymore and I got up and ran down the hall to the kitchen. There, in the middle of the room, wearing his Goodyear jacket and work clothes, was my father. He was on his hands and knees, his head hanging as though it were too heavy to support, and he was rocking back and forth and babbling in a rhythmic stutter. It's funny, but the first thing I thought when I saw him like that was the way he used to give me rides on his back, when I was little, bucking and neighing like a horse. And as soon as I thought it, I felt my heart lurch in my chest. "Dad?" I said. "What's wrong?" But he didn't hear me. I went over to him then. "Dad?" I said again, and touched him on the shoulder. He jerked at the touch and looked up at me, his lips moving but no sounds coming out of them now. His forehead was knotted and his eyes were red, almost raw-looking. He swallowed hard and for the first time spoke words I could recognize, though I did not understand them until years later, when I was myself a father.

"Danny," he said. "Save me."

Before I could finish dialing the school lunchroom's number, my mother pulled into the driveway. Looking out the window, I saw her jump out of the car and run up the slick sidewalk, her camel-colored overcoat open and flapping in the wind. For a moment I was confused. Had I already called her? How much time had passed since I found my father on the kitchen floor? A minute? An hour? Then I realized that someone else must have told her something was wrong.

She burst in the back door then and called out, "Bill? Bill? Are you here?"

"Mom," I said, "Dad's—" and then I didn't know how to finish the sentence.

She came in the kitchen without stopping to remove her galoshes. "Oh, Bill," she said when she saw us, "are you all right?"

My father was sitting at the kitchen table now, his hands fluttering in his lap. A few moments before, I had helped him to his feet and, draping his arm over my shoulders, led him to the table like a wounded man.

"Helen," he said. "It's you." He said it as if he hadn't seen her for years.

My mother went over and knelt beside him. "I'm so sorry," she said, but whether that statement was born of sorrow over something she had said or done or whether she just simply and guiltlessly wished he weren't suffering, I never knew. Taking his hands in hers, she added, "There's nothing to worry about. Everything's going to be fine." Then she turned to me. Her brown hair was wind-blown, and her face was so pale the smudges of rouge on her cheeks looked like bruises. "Danny," she said, "I want you to leave us alone for a few minutes."

I looked at her red-rimmed eyes and tight lips. "Okay," I said, and went back to the living room. There, I sat on the sagging couch and stared at the television, the actors' mouths moving wordlessly, their laughs eerily silent. I could hear my parents talking, their steady murmur broken from time to time by my father sobbing and my mother saying "Bill" over and over, in the tone mothers use to calm their babies, but I couldn't hear enough of what they said to know what had happened. And I didn't *want* to know either. I wanted them to be as silent as the people on the TV, I wanted all the words to stop, all the crying.

I lay down and closed my eyes, trying to drive the picture of my father on the kitchen floor out of my head. My heart was beating so hard I could feel my pulse tick in my throat. I was worried about my father but I was also angry that he was acting so strange. It didn't seem fair that I had to have a father like that. I'd never seen anybody else's father act that way, not even in a movie.

Outside, the wind shook the evergreens and every now and then a gust would rattle the windowpane. I lay there a long time, listening to the wind, until my heart stopped beating so hard.

Sometime later, my mother came into the room and sat on the edge of the chair under the sunburst mirror. Her forehead was creased, and there were black mascara streaks on her cheeks. Leaning toward me, her hands clasped, she bit her lip, then said, "I just wanted to tell you not to worry. Everything's going to be all right." Her breath snagged on the last word, and I could hear her swallowing.

"What's wrong?" I asked.

She opened her mouth as if she were about to answer, but suddenly her eyes began to tear. "We'll talk about it later," she said. "After the doctor's come. Just don't worry, okay? I'll explain everything."

"The doctor?" I said.

"I'll explain later," she answered.

Then she left and I didn't hear anything more until ten or fifteen minutes had passed and the doorbell rang. My mother ran to the door and opened it, and I heard her say, "Thank you for coming so quickly. He's in the kitchen." As they hurried down the hall past the living room, I caught a glimpse of Dr. Lewis and his black leather bag. It had been years since the doctors in our town, small as it was, made house calls, so I knew now that my father's problem was something truly serious. The word *emergency* came into my mind, and though I tried to push it out, it kept coming back.

For the next half hour or so, I stayed in the living room, listening to the droning sound of Dr. Lewis and my parents talking. I still didn't know what had happened or why. All I knew was that my father was somebody else now, somebody I didn't know. I tried to reconcile the man who used to read to me at night when my mother was too tired, the man who patiently taught me how to measure and cut plywood for a birdhouse, even the man whose cheeks twitched when he was angry at me and whose silences were suffocating, with the man I had just seen crouched like an animal on the kitchen floor babbling some incomprehensible language. But I couldn't. And though I felt sorry for him and his suffering, I felt as much shame as sympathy. *This is your father*, I told myself. *This is you when you're older.*

It wasn't until after Dr. Lewis had left and my father had taken the tranquilizers and gone upstairs to bed that my mother came back into the living room, sat down on the couch beside me, and told me what had happened. "Your father," she began, and her voice cracked. Then she controlled herself and said, "Your father has been fired from his job."

I looked at her. "Is that it?" I said. "That's what all this fuss is about?" I couldn't believe he'd put us through all this for something so unimportant. All he had to do was get a new job. What was the big deal?

"Let me explain," my mother said. "He was fired some time ago. Ten days ago, to be exact. But he hadn't said anything to me about it, and he just kept on getting up and going down to work every morning, like nothing had happened. And every day Mr. Siverhus told him to leave, and after arguing a while, he'd go. Then he'd spend the rest of the day driving around until quitting time, when he'd finally come home. But Mr. Siverhus got fed up and changed the locks, and when your father came to work today he couldn't get in. He tried all three entrances, and when he found his key didn't work in any of them, well, he threw a trash barrel through the showroom window and went inside."

She paused for a moment, I think to see how I was taking this. I was trying to picture my father throwing a barrel through that huge, expensive window. It wasn't easy to imagine. Even at his most angry, he had never been violent. He had never even threatened to hit me or my mother. But now he'd broken a window, and the law.

My mother went on. "Then when he was inside, he found that Mr. Siverhus had changed the lock on his office too, so he kicked the door in. When Mr. Siverhus came to work, he found your dad sitting at his desk, going over service accounts." Her lips started to tremble. "He could have called the police," she said, "but he called me instead. We owe him for that."

That's the story my mother told me. Though I was to find out later that she hadn't told me the entire truth, she had told me enough of it to make me realize that my father had gone crazy. Something in him—whatever slender idea or feeling it is that connects us to the world—had broken, and he was not in the world anymore, he was outside it, horribly outside it, and could not get back in no matter how he tried. Somehow I knew this, even then. And I wondered if someday the same thing would happen to me.

The rest of that day, I stayed downstairs, watching TV or reading *Sports Illustrated* or *Life*, while my father slept or rested. My mother sat beside his bed, reading her ladies magazines while he slept and talking to him whenever he woke, and every now and then she came downstairs to tell me he was doing fine. She spoke as if he had some temporary fever, some twenty-four-hour virus, that would be gone by morning.

But the next morning, a Saturday, my father was still not himself. He didn't feel like coming down for breakfast, so she made him scrambled eggs, sausage, and toast and took it up to him on a tray. He hadn't eaten since the previous morning, but when she came back down awhile later all the food was still on the tray. She didn't say anything about the untouched meal; she just said my father wanted to talk to me.

"I can't," I said. "I'm eating." I had one sausage patty and a few bites of scrambled egg left on my plate.

"Not this minute," she said. "When you're done."

I looked out the window. It had been snowing all morning, and the evergreens in the backyard looked like flocked

Christmas trees waiting for strings of colored lights. Some sparrows were flying in and out of the branches, chirping, and others were lined up on the crossbars of the clothesline poles, their feathers fluffed out and blowing in the wind.

"I'm supposed to meet Rob at his house," I lied. "I'll be late."

"Danny," she said, in a way that warned me not to make her say any more.

"All right," I said, and I shoved my plate aside and got up. "But I don't have much time."

Upstairs, I stopped at my father's closed door. Normally I would have walked right in, but that day I felt I should knock. I felt as if I were visiting a stranger. Even his room— I didn't think of it as belonging to my mother anymore— seemed strange, somehow separate from the rest of the house.

When I knocked, my father said, "Is that you, Danny?" and I stepped inside. All the blinds were shut, and the dim air smelled like a thick, musty mixture of hair tonic and Aqua Velva. My father was sitting on the edge of his un-made bed, wearing his old brown robe, nubbled from years of washings, and maroon corduroy slippers. His face was blotchy, and his eyes were dark and pouched.

"Mom said you wanted to talk to me," I said.

He touched a spot next to him on the bed. "Here. Sit down."

I didn't move. "I've got to go to Rob's," I said.

He cleared his throat and looked away. For a moment we were silent, and I could hear the heat register ticking.

"I just wanted to tell you to take good care of your mother," he said then.

I shifted my weight from one foot to the other. "What do you mean?"

He looked back at me, his gaze steady and empty, and I wondered how much of the way he was that moment was his medication and how much himself. "She needs someone to take care of her," he said. "That's all."

"What about you? Aren't you going to take care of her anymore?"

He cleared his throat again. "If I can."

"I don't get it," I said. "Why are you doing this to us? What's going on?"

"Nothing's going on," he answered. "That's the problem. Not a thing is going on."

"I don't know what you mean. I don't like it when you say things I can't understand."

"I don't like it either," he said. Then he added: "That wasn't me yesterday. I want you to know that."

"It sure looked like you. If it wasn't you, who was it then?"

He stood up and walked across the carpet to the window. But he didn't open the blinds; he just stood there, his back to me. "It's all right for you to be mad," he said.

"I'm not mad."

"Don't lie, Danny."

"I'm not lying. I just like my father to use the English language when he talks to me, that's all."

For a long moment he was quiet. It seemed almost as if he'd forgotten I was in the room. Then he said, "My grandmother used to tell me there were exactly as many stars in the sky as there were people. If someone was born, there'd be a new star in the sky that night, and you could find it if you looked hard enough. And if someone died, you'd see that person's star fall."

"What are you talking about?" I said.

"People," he answered. "Stars."

Then he just stood there, staring at the blinds. I wondered if he was seeing stars there, or his grandmother, or what. And all of a sudden I felt my throat close up and my eyes start to sting. I was surprised—a moment before I'd been so angry, but now I was almost crying.

I tried to swallow, but I couldn't. I wanted to know what was wrong, so I could know how to feel about it; I wanted to be sad or angry, either one, but not both at the same time. "What *happened*?" I finally said. "*Tell* me."

He turned, but I wasn't sure he'd heard me, because he didn't answer for a long time. And when he did, he seemed to be answering some other question, one I hadn't asked.

"I was so arrogant," he said. "I thought my life would work out."

I stood there looking at him. "I don't understand."

"I hope you never do," he said. "I hope to God you never do."

"Quit talking like that."

"Like what?"

"Like you're so *smart* and everything. Like you're above all of this when it's you that's causing it all."

He looked down at the floor and shook his head slowly.

"Well?" I said. "Aren't you going to say something?"

He looked up. "You're a good boy, Danny. I'm proud of you. I wish I could be a better father for you."

I hesitate now to say what I said next. But then I didn't hesitate.

"So do I," I said bitterly. "So the hell do I." And I turned to leave.

"Danny, wait," my father said.

But I didn't wait. And when I shut the door, I shut it hard.

Two days later, after he took to fits of weeping and laughing, we drove my father to the VA hospital in Minneapolis. Dr. Lewis had already called the hospital and made arrangements for his admission, so we were quickly escorted to his room on the seventh floor, where the psychiatric patients were kept. I had expected the psych ward to be a dreary, prisonlike place with barred doors and gray, windowless walls, but if anything, it was cheerier than the rest of the hospital. There were sky blue walls in the hallway, hung here and there with watercolor landscapes the patients had painted, and sunny yellow walls in the rooms, and there was a brightly lit lounge with a TV, card tables, and a shelf full of board games, and even a crafts center where the patients could do decoupage, leatherwork, mosaics, and macramé. And the patients we saw looked so normal that I almost wondered whether we were in the right place. Most of them were older, probably veterans of the First World War, but a few were my father's age or younger. The old ones were the friendliest, nodding their bald heads or waving their liver-spotted hands as we passed, but even those who only looked at us seemed pleasant or, at the least, not hostile.

I was relieved by what I saw but evidently my father was not, for his eyes still had the quicksilver shimmer of fear they'd had all during the drive from Glencoe. He sat stiffly in the wheelchair and looked at the floor passing between his feet as the big-boned nurse pushed him down the hall toward his room.

We were lucky, the nurse told us, chatting away in a strange accent, which I later learned was Czech. There had been only one private room left, and my father had gotten it. And it had a *lovely* view of the hospital grounds. Sometimes she herself would stand in front of that window and watch the snow fall on the birches and park benches. It was such a beautiful sight. She asked my father if that didn't sound nice, but he didn't answer.

Then she wheeled him into the room and parked the chair beside the white, starched-looking bed. My father hadn't wanted to sit in the chair when we checked him in at the admissions desk, but now he didn't show any desire to get out of it.

"Well, what do you think of your room, Mr. Conroy?" the nurse asked. My mother stood beside her, a handkerchief squeezed in her hand.

My father looked at the chrome railing on the bed, the stainless steel tray beside it, and the plastic-sealed water glasses on the tray. Then he looked at my mother and me.

"I suppose it's where I should be," he said.

During the five weeks my father was in the hospital, my mother drove to Minneapolis twice a week to visit him. Despite her urgings, I refused to go with her. I wanted to forget about my father, to erase him from my life. But I didn't tell her that. I told her I couldn't stand to see him in that awful place, and she felt sorry for me and let me stay home. But almost every time she came back, she'd have a gift for me from him: a postcard of Minnehaha Falls decoupaged onto a walnut plaque, a leather billfold with my initials burned into the cover, a belt decorated with turquoise and white beads. And a request: would I come see him that weekend? But I never went.

Glencoe was a small town, and like all small towns it was devoted to gossip. I knew my classmates had heard about my father—many of them had no doubt driven past Goodyear to see the broken window the way they'd drive past a body shop to see a car that had been totaled—but only Rob said anything. When he asked what had happened, I told him what Dr. Lewis had told me, that my father was just overworked and exhausted. Rob didn't believe me any more than I believed Dr. Lewis, but he pretended to accept that explanation. I wasn't sure if I liked him more for that pretense, or less.

It took a couple of weeks for the gossip to reach me. One day during lunch Rob told me that Todd Knutson, whose father was a mechanic at Goodyear, was telling everybody my father had been fired for embezzling. "I know it's a dirty lie," Rob said, "but some kids think he's telling the truth, so you'd better do something."

"Like what?" I said.

"Tell them the truth. Set the record straight."

I looked at my friend's earnest, acne-scarred face. As soon as he'd told me the rumor, I'd known it was true, and in my heart I had already convicted my father. But I didn't want my best friend to know that. Perhaps I was worried that he would turn against me too and I'd be completely alone.

"You bet I will," I said. "I'll make him eat those words."

But I had no intention of defending my father. I was already planning to go see Mr. Siverhus right after school and ask him, straight out, for the truth, so I could confront my father with the evidence and shame him the way he had shamed me. I was furious with him for making me even more of an outcast than I had been—I was the son of a *criminal* now—and I wanted to make him pay for it. All during my afternoon classes, I imagined going to see him at the hospital and telling him I knew his secret. He'd deny it at first, I was sure, but as soon as he saw I knew everything, he'd confess. He'd beg my forgiveness, swearing he'd never do anything to embarrass me or my mother again, but nothing he could say would make any difference—I'd just turn and walk away. And if I were called into court to testify against him, I'd take the stand and swear to tell the whole truth and nothing but the truth, my eyes steady on him all the while, watching him sit there beside his lawyer, his head hung, speechless.

I was angry at my mother too, because she hadn't told me everything. But I didn't realize until that afternoon, when I drove down to Goodyear to see Mr. Siverhus, just how much she hadn't told me.

Mr. Siverhus was a tall, silver-haired man who looked more like a banker than the manager of a tire store. He was wearing a starched white shirt, a blue-and-gray striped tie with a silver tie tack, and iridescent sharkskin trousers, and when he shook my hand he smiled so hard his crow's-feet almost hid his eyes. He led me into his small but meticulous office, closing the door on the smell of grease and the noise of impact wrenches removing lugs from wheels, and I blurted out my question before either of us even sat down.

"Who told you that?" he asked.

"My mother," I answered. I figured he wouldn't lie to me if he thought my mother had already told me the truth. Then I asked him again: "Is it true?"

Mr. Siverhus didn't answer right away. Instead, he gestured toward a chair opposite his gray metal desk and waited until I sat in it. Then he pushed some carefully stacked papers aside, sat on the edge of the desk, and asked me how my father was doing. I didn't really know—my mother kept saying he was getting better, but I wasn't sure I could believe her. Still, I said, "Fine."

He nodded. "I'm glad to hear that," he said. "I'm really terribly sorry about everything that's happened. I hope you and your mother know that."

He wanted me to say something, but I didn't. Standing up, he wandered over to the gray file cabinet and looked out the window at the showroom, where the new tires and batteries were on display. He sighed, and I knew he didn't want to be having this conversation.

"What your mother told you is true," he said then. "Bill was taking money. Not much, you understand, but enough that it soon became obvious we had a problem. After some investigating, we found out he was the one. I couldn't have been more surprised. Your father had been a loyal and hardworking employee for years, and he was the last person I would've expected to be stealing from us. But when we confronted him with it, he admitted it. He'd been having trouble making his mortgage payments, he said, and in a weak moment he'd taken some money and, later on, a little more. He seemed genuinely sorry about it and he swore he'd pay back every cent, so we gave him another chance."

"But he did it again, didn't he?" I said.

I don't know if Mr. Siverhus noticed the anger shaking my voice or not. He just looked at me and let out a slow breath. "Yes," he said sadly. "He did. And so I had to fire him. I told him we wouldn't prosecute if he returned the money, and he promised he would."

Then he went behind his desk and sat down heavily in his chair. "I hope you understand."

"I'm not blaming you," I said. "*You* didn't do anything wrong."

He leaned over the desk toward me. "I appreciate that," he said. "You don't know how badly I've felt about all of this. I keep thinking that maybe I should have handled it differently. I don't know, when I think that he might have taken his life because of this, well, I—"

"Taken his life?" I interrupted.

Mr. Siverhus sat back in his chair. "Your mother didn't tell you?"

I shook my head and closed my eyes for a second. I felt as if something had broken loose in my chest and risen into my throat, making it hard to breathe, to think.

"I assumed you knew," he said. "I'm sorry, I shouldn't have said anything."

"Tell me," I said.

"I think you'd better talk to your mother about this, Danny. I don't think I should be the one to tell you."

"I need to know," I said.

Mr. Siverhus looked at me for a long moment. Then he said, "Very well. But you have to realize that your father was under a lot of stress. I'm sure that by the time he gets out of the hospital, he'll be back to normal, and you won't ever have to worry about him getting like that again."

I nodded. I didn't believe him, but I wanted him to go on.

Mr. Siverhus took a deep breath and let it out slowly. "When I came to work that morning and found your father in his office, he had a gun in his hand. A revolver. At first, I thought he was going to shoot me. But then he put it up to his own head. I tell you, I was scared. 'Bill,' I said, 'that's not the answer.' And then I just kept talking. It took me ten or fifteen minutes to get him to put the gun down. Then he left, and that's when I called your mother."

I must have had a strange look on my face because the next thing he said was, "Are you all right?"

I nodded, but I wasn't all right. I felt woozy, as if I'd just discovered another world inside this one, a world that made this one false. I wanted to leave, but I wasn't sure I could stand up. Then I did.

"Thank you, Mr. Siverhus," I said, and reached out to shake his hand. I wanted to say more but there was nothing to say. I turned and left.

Outside in the parking lot, I stood beside the Chevy, looking at the new showroom window and breathing in the cold. I was thinking how, only a few months before, I had been looking through my father's dresser for his old army uniform, which I wanted to wear to Rob's Halloween party, and I'd found the revolver tucked under his dress khakis in the bottom drawer. My father had always been full of warnings—don't mow the lawn barefoot, never go swimming in a river, always drive defensively—but he had never even mentioned he owned this gun, much less warned me not to touch it. I wondered why, and I held the gun up to the light, as if I could somehow see through it to an understanding of its meaning. But I couldn't—or at least I refused to believe that I could—and I put it back exactly where I found it and never mentioned it to anyone.

I didn't tell my mother what I had learned from Mr. Siverhus, and I didn't tell anyone else either. After dinner that night I went straight to my room and stayed there. I wanted to be alone, to figure things out, but the more I thought, the more I didn't know what to think. I wondered if it was starting already, if I was already going crazy like my father, because I wasn't sure who I was or what I felt. It had been a long time since I'd prayed, but that night I prayed that when I woke the next day everything would make sense again.

But the next morning I was still in a daze. Everything seemed so false, so disconnected from the real world I had glimpsed the day before, that I felt disoriented, almost dizzy. At school, the chatter of my classmates sounded as meaningless as my father's babble, and everything I saw seemed out of focus, distorted, the way things do just before you faint. Walking down the hall, I saw Todd Knutson standing by his locker, talking with Bonnie Zempel, a friend of Molly Rasmussen's, and suddenly I found myself walking up to them. I didn't know what I was going to say or do, I hadn't planned anything, and when I shoved Todd against his locker, it surprised me as much as it did him.

"I hope you're happy now," I said to him. "My father *died* last night." I'm not sure I can explain it now, but in a way I believed what I was saying, and my voice shook with a genuine grief.

Todd slowly lowered his fists. "What?" he said, and looked quickly at Bonnie's startled, open face.

"He had *cancer*," I said, biting down on the word to keep my mind from whirling. "A tumor on his brain. That's why he did the things he did, taking that money and breaking that window and everything. He couldn't help it."

And then my grief was too much for me, and I turned and strode down the hall, tears coming into my eyes. I waited until I was around the corner and out of their sight, then I started running, as fast as I could. Only then did I come back into the world and wonder what I had done.

That afternoon, my mother appeared at the door of my algebra class in her blue uniform and black hair net. At first I thought she was going to embarrass me by waving at me, as she often did when she happened to pass one of my classrooms, but then I saw the look on her face. "Excuse me, Mr. Laughlin," she said grimly, "I'm sorry to interrupt your class but I need to speak with my son for a moment."

Mr. Laughlin turned his dour face from the blackboard, his stick of chalk suspended in mid-calculation, and said, "Certainly, Mrs. Conroy. I hope there's nothing the matter."

"No," she said. "It's nothing to worry about."

But out in the hall, she slapped my face hard.

"How *dare* you say your father is dead," she said through clenched teeth. Her gray eyes were flinty and narrow.

"I didn't," I answered.

She raised her hand and slapped me again, even harder this time.

"Don't you lie to me, Daniel."

I started to cry. "Well, I wish he *was*," I said. "I wish he was dead, so all of this could be over."

My mother raised her hand again, but then she let it fall. "Go," she said. "Get away from me. I can't bear to look at you another minute."

I went back into the classroom and sat down. I felt awful about hurting my mother, but not so awful that I wasn't worried whether my classmates had heard her slap me or noticed my burning cheek. I saw them looking at me and shaking their heads, heard them whispering and laughing under their breath, and I stood up, my head roiling, and asked if I could be excused.

Mr. Laughlin looked at me. Then, without even asking what was wrong, he wrote out a pass to the nurse's office and handed it to me. As I left the room, I heard him say to the class, "That's enough. If I hear one more remark..."

Later, lying on a cot in the nurse's office, my hands folded over my chest, I closed my eyes and imagined I was dead and my parents and classmates were kneeling before my open coffin, their heads bowed in mourning.

After that day, my mother scheduled meetings for me with Father Ondahl, our priest, and Mr. Jenseth, the school counselor. She said she hoped they could help me through this difficult time, then added, "Obviously, I can't." I saw Father Ondahl two or three times, and as soon as I assured him that I still had my faith, though I did not, he said I'd be better off just seeing Mr. Jenseth from then on. I saw Mr.

Jenseth three times a week for the next month, then once a week for the rest of the school year. I'm not sure how those meetings helped, or even if they did. All I know is that, in time, my feelings about my father, and about myself, changed.

My mother continued her visits to my father, but she no longer asked me to go along with her, and when she came home from seeing him, she waited until I asked before she'd tell me how he was. I wondered whether she'd told him I was seeing a counselor, and why, but I didn't dare ask. And I wondered if she'd ever forgive me for my terrible lie.

Then one day, without telling me beforehand, she returned from Minneapolis with my father. "Danny," she called, and I came out of the living room and saw them in the entryway. My father was stamping the snow off his black wingtips, and he had a suitcase in one hand and a watercolor of our house in the other, the windows yellow with light and a thin swirl of gray smoke rising from the red brick chimney. He looked pale and even thinner than I remembered. I was so surprised to see him, all I could say was "You're home."

"That's right," he said, and put down the suitcase and painting. "The old man's back." Then he tried to smile, but it came out more like a wince. I knew he wanted me to hug him and say how happy I was to see him, and part of me wanted to do that, too. But I didn't. I just shook his hand as I would have an uncle's or a stranger's, then picked up the painting and looked at it.

"This is nice," I said. "Real nice."

"I'm glad you like it," he answered.

And then we just stood there until my mother said, "Well, let's get you unpacked, dear, and then we can all sit down and talk."

Despite everything that had happened, our life together after that winter was relatively peaceful. My father got a job at Firestone, and though for years he barely made enough to meet expenses, eventually he worked his way up to assistant manager and earned a good living. He occasionally lost his temper and succumbed to self-pity as he always had, but for the rest of his life, he was as normal and sane as anybody. Perhaps Dr. Lewis had been right after all, and all my father had needed was a good rest. In any case, by the time I was grown and married myself, his breakdown seemed a strange and impossible dream and I wondered, as I watched him play with my infant son, if I hadn't imagined some of it. It amazed me that a life could break so utterly, then mend itself.

But of course it had not mended entirely, as my life had also not mended entirely. There was a barrier between us, the thin but indestructible memory of what we had been to each other that winter. I was never sure just how much he knew about the way I'd felt about him then, or even whether my mother had told him my lie about his death, but I knew he was aware that I hadn't been a good son. Perhaps the barrier between us could have been broken with a single word—the word *love* or its synonym *forgive*—but as if by mutual pact we never spoke of that difficult winter or its consequences.

Only once did we come close to discussing it. He and my mother had come to visit me and my family in Minneapolis, and we had just finished our Sunday dinner. Caroline and my mother were clearing the table, Sam was playing on the kitchen floor with the dump truck my parents had bought him for his birthday, and my father and I were sitting in the living room watching *60 Minutes*. The black pastor of a Pentecostal church in Texas was talking to Morley Safer about "the Spirit that descends upon us and inhabits our hearts." Then the camera cut to a black woman standing in the midst of a clapping congregation, her eyes tightly closed and her face glowing with sweat as she rocked back and forth, speaking the incoherent language of angels or demons. Her syllables rose and fell, then mounted in a syntax of spiraling rapture until finally, overcome by the voice that had spoken through her, she sank to her knees, trembling, her eyes open and glistening. The congregation clapped harder then, some of them leaping and dancing as if their bodies were lifted by the collapse of hers, and they yelled, "Praise God!" and "Praise the Lord God Almighty!"

I glanced at my father, who sat watching this with a blank face, and wondered what he was thinking. Then, when the camera moved to another Pentecostal minister discussing a transcript of the woman's speech, a transcript he claimed contained variations on ancient Hebrew and Aramaic words she couldn't possibly have known, I turned to him and asked, in a hesitant way, whether he wanted to keep watching or change channels.

My father's milky blue eyes looked blurred, as if he were looking at something a long way off, and he cleared his throat before he spoke. "It's up to you," he said. "Do you want to watch it?"

I paused. Then I said, "No," and changed the channel.

Perhaps if I had said yes, we might have talked about that terrible day he put a gun to his head and I could have told him what I had since grown to realize—that I loved him. That I had always loved him, though behind his back, without letting him know it. And, in a way, behind *my* back, too. But I didn't say yes, and in the seven years that remained of his life, we never came as close to ending the winter that was always, for us, an unspoken but living part of our present.

That night, though, unable to sleep, I got up and went into my son's room. Standing there in the wan glow of his night light, I listened to him breathe for a while, then quietly took down the railing we'd put on his bed to keep him from rolling off and hurting himself. Then I sat on the edge of the bed and began to stroke his soft, reddish blond hair. At first he didn't wake, but his forehead wrinkled and he mumbled a little dream-sound.

I am not a religious man. I believe, as my father must have, the day he asked me to save him, that our children are our only salvation, their love our only redemption. And that night, when my son woke, frightened by the dark figure leaning over him, and started to cry, I picked him up and rocked him in my arms, comforting him as I would after a nightmare. "Don't worry," I told him over and over, until the words sounded as incomprehensible to me as they must have to him, "it's only a dream. Everything's going to be all right. Don't worry."

Cadence

by Erica Plouffe Lazure

Something ate a hole through the oil tank, so we called Joey in from the pumps to fix it. The tank had been drained, mostly, but mostly never helped no one. Joey didn't have gloves, just some rubber goggles, and this one time nobody told him to go and get the good mask. He could've found the cat litter in the closet, could've poured it in first to absorb what we'd left in there, but he didn't do that either. It probably wouldn't have helped. Even with those goggles on, he would've seen the ember that strayed through the hole, the welding rod still pinched between his fingers, the little spark that built the flame that rocked us all to the back of the bay.

The body looks strange on fire. It's just everywhere at once, liquid and growing, Joey tearing out toward the nasty patch of grass on Highway Eleven with flames eating through his skin. And we just stood there stupid, like disciples struck, helpless except for a woman waiting for an oil change who called 9-1-1 from our pay phone. But what were we supposed to do? He was gone, and we all knew it, except maybe for Mr. Andy Arlen, moving too late from behind his desk, belly-heavy in work boots, extinguisher in hand. The fire was out already. Joey was blind and smoldering with snuffed heat on that small strip of highway lawn, me kneeling nearby telling him the things he'd want to hear in his last few moments, cars still pulling in to the station. And Mr. Goddamn Fucking Hero Arlen pushing through with his cherry-red tank, the pin pulled—it made me wish, as the foam hit and Joey screamed his last, that Mr. Arlen had stayed behind his goddamned desk. He stood over Joey holding the tank like he'd just taken the world's biggest pressurized piss. That's when I threw up.

In all the years I knew him, Joey was never one to just let a subject be. And for the past month he'd been nonstop about his girl Becky in Basic. When she left for the Army he went on and on about the mix tape he'd made for her, the magazines he'd bought her, the fudge his mother made, the jumbo pack of Skittles he'd found at Sam's Club, the troll doll with camouflage hair and pants to match. He liked to tell me all about her "particular brand of fucking," as he'd called it, specialty moves of hers that I knew only too well. So well that I knew when he started to make stuff up. He didn't write many letters; he was more of a candy-and-flowers man. He'd sit at the station between pump calls and write a few I-miss-you's on yellow lined paper. And just last week he told me how the Skittles and the fudge and the mix tape and the rest of it was banned anyway.

"What she got," he said, "was one good look at all the things I'd sent her. Then her sergeant took it away. Worse than me not sending it at all."

Becky has good features but bad skin that she tries to hide with beige makeup. She keeps at least three bottles of that stuff in her bathroom. I've seen it. Contour, she calls it. It works better at night, or in the dark, at bars a few towns over. Becky's barroom eyeliner makes you forget about those bottles of pancake in her bathroom, makes you forget how a close hug from her will more than likely leave a tan rash on your T-shirt. A few years back Becky Barker was co-captain superstar forward of the Lady Tigers, came close to a scoring record. Barker's been a big name in high school field hockey since her older sisters played.

But the first time she took me home she was already over all that. She had a thread of green dental floss strung across her left breast, stuck to the nubs of her sweater, clinging like tinsel to the pilled part below her shoulder, and she gave me one of those hidden, rim-of-the-eye smiles when I asked about her hygiene technique. "Gotta keep the girls plaque-free somehow," she said. She told me she'd started young in the bars, nabbing one of her big sisters' IDs when she was seventeen. No one ever called her on it, even though her picture was in all the papers that season. Ask me, that four-year jumpstart on bar life kept with her and there she was at twenty-four at the same bar looking at least thirty under all that makeup.

Becky's been writing to me since her first week at Basic, saying from the start how she wished she'd wrapped it up with Joey before she left. How she wants me instead of him. How the one thing Basic fails to train you for is what to do with the life you leave back in Mewborn. Last week she said Joey had one more letter coming, and then she'd be free for me, for real. She told me to watch for it, made me promise to talk to him if he brought it up. She said, "My sergeant says, 'The more you carry, the more you carry.' I don't have room for a troll doll, anyway."

And so I wasted the whole morning looking for clues in his face. At Burger King I waited for him to say something about her, because that was my cue, my lead-in to let him know his personal business with Becky was mine, too. I could see the folded note in the pocket of his T-shirt, the telltale border on the envelope. But he just ate his burger with fries and talked about Friday's game at the high school like nothing had changed, like Becky was still scoring points in her plaid skirt and mouth guard. I waited for it all day and he said not a word, not a word until the spark hit that puddle of oil. Not until he was down on the ground with no face, me kneeling next to him—that's when he talked, right before Arlen came barreling through with his goddamn superman extinguisher. I heard him.

Becky's got a month left of Basic, and then it's off to Aberdeen for ordnance training. Between the training is two weeks at home. She's thinking about going Airborne so she can nab a Fort Bragg assignment, so there'd be but an hour between us. She picked ordnance, she said, because she loves dogs, even the bomb-sniffing ones. She's hinted more than once I should think about a move to Fayetteville. Even though she's in South Carolina and on her way to Maryland. Even though it's the Bragg soldiers they're shipping daily overseas. Even though I wasn't sure I wanted Becky in-the-Daylight. Becky out-of-bars. Becky out-of-bed. I wrote her as much using nicer words, said I wasn't sure I was worth jumping out of a plane for. But I said I'd talk to Joey if she talked to him first.

But then Joey died. I saw him tear across our lot with the welder still on. The oil tank scattered across the bay in white-hot pieces. Bits of it kicked into his skin, turned him to blue fire in seconds. He cooked the palms of his hands trying to pry the goggles from his face.

The rules change after a fuel tank explodes and eyelids burn away and tear ducts are gone and you're kneeling beside your best friend and his face and body have no skin. Becky would understand. In Basic they tell each other stories that end like this, best friends and fire and all. Knowing her, she'll listen to every track on that tape Joey made. She'll make me come pick her up at Fort Jackson and I'll have to hear it all the way home. And at some point, she'll loosen my grip from the stick shift and hold my hand in her lap and won't say a thing about what happened. She'll collar me with her silence and grief and guilt as "Tumbling Dice" moves through us, and that's when I'll know that I'm hers now, that this is the way she'll pull us into public. At Joey's funeral they'll play "I'll be There for You" straight from the tape and she'll appear in her dress uniform and claim her place as Grieving Girlfriend, and I'll be the Grieving Best Friend and his parents will be real nice to both of us and won't it make sense to everyone for us to find comfort together in our loss? It's just what he would have wanted, she'll tell me, me finishing with her what Joey could not. And how cheap would it be to tell her what a farce that mix tape really is, how Joey borrowed more than half my tape collection and then used my boom box to make it? It's not worth upstaging someone after they're dead.

Which is why she won't ask what we talked about. Which is why I won't tell her that when I knelt by Joey and told him about Becky in her boots, marching across a swamp in South Carolina, clutching a map, finding a coordinate, on her way back to him, Arlen almost there with the extinguisher, I swear I heard him say it. "I know," he said. "I know."

And what do *I* know? It was nobody's fault. Even when I thought about what might happen down the line, to her out there and Joey here and me in between, I saw it all working itself out. I didn't see myself looking at what's left of Joey. I didn't see me losing him and her getting me. I still don't see it.

"Cadence" originally appeared in *McSweeney's #29*.

Blue of the World

by Douglas W. Milliken

May 24th, 1965

Walked the orchard line with the boy today after the service, from the house to the north end of the property. All the blooms had blown off the limbs so just a foamy wash of white or dried-up yellow petals were left here and there on the ground. Very many small green apples have started, few much bigger than the head of a nail. The trees looked good. I do not much fear a late frost ruining everything that's begun. But in this, I've been wrong before.

The land very slightly inclines to the north here so it was harder going up than coming back. We collected blowdowns as we followed the single straight file of trees, stacking them on a sledge the boy pulled. I brought a saw in case we needed to clear a split limb from a live tree. We needed the saw twice. Mules grazed nearby with the jack donkey in the pasture east of us and after a spell, were joined by the quarter horses. We'd been discovered. Just post and board fence between us and them, they following as we worked the orchard line. We must have been good fun to watch. I suggested we hitch the sledge to any one of them—it's easy work for a horse and not work at all for a mule—but the boy said no.

The pasture west of the orchard has grown meadow-sweet and fallow with tall grass. If I can mend the fences on that side of the trees, I will swap the beasts over there. But I'm not certain I have that ambition yet this year.

At the northern boundary line where our land meets the Finnegans', we rested and ate sandwiches and shared cold coffee from a jelly jar. We agreed, the coffee was not as good as it used to be. Something missing, or the ratios wrong. It's hard to enjoy a thing when your memory of it is sweeter. Toward the far away hills, men were standing the first girders of a new weather tower. The sight of it makes me hate. We finished our lunch and coffee and headed back south to the house, looking for anything we missed along the way. The horses followed.

May 25th, 1965

Taught the boy how to mend the leather of a stirrup torn free from its fender. He is still too short to work at the bench with ease.

May 28th, 1965

John Henneker has called everyday for the past two weeks, begging me to bring a sire out to rut his dam Dilly, and only just yesterday offered to pay me for this service. Being neighbors entitles us to nothing of each other. He must have just got the news. He named what he could pay and I told him what that could buy him. He didn't seem too picky. Chose a young painted stud, barely more than a colt.

Never been sired. Quick and leggy. Rambunctious and maybe a little dumb. It all sounded fine to John. All he asked is that it be pretty.

The Henneker farm is a twenty mile drive or more but only fifteen if one draws a straight line between our two places, and anyway they weren't expecting us at any particular time, so the boy and I saddled up our Ghost and Coyote before dawn and led the paint by a rope from the team. Among the wild parti-colors of quarter horses, there's a wordless rare something in riding tall milk-white Saddlebreds. It's best in the dark before sunrise, when you're the only white thing in the world glowing like a moon. It's good to feel you're a rare riding thing sometimes, even if you aren't. We took turns holding the paint's rope: when we crossed a property, we'd switch. Headed north along the orchard line and crossed onto the Finnegans' land, down their pasture and through the wooded way and along the west shore of their wide, muddy cattle pond, then up the grassy slope and across a dirt road onto the Halls' land where things flatten and dry out nicely. It's a piece of land that'd be more at home two hundred miles west of here, in Interior or Kadoka. No good for pasture or growing much more than pigweed and morning glory and really, given the rockiness, not the safest riding. A horse can twist an ankle on a loose stone as easily as a man can. But it feels correct. The sun was still low so the earth looked more purple and blue than anything else. Now and then, a spooked rabbit would dart off ahead of us and disappear. It was ghostly, that flash of rabbit. Far away, we could see the big hills rolling. The boy had once said they looked like someone lying with a blanket pulled up over her face. But he didn't say anything today. Told him, back east, people called these mountains. He said he knew, I'd told him that before.

We took the horses easy on that sweet flat piece, then watered them at Cane Brook. That marked the boundary between the Halls' and Hennekers' lands. But we still had a ways to go. We traded the paint's rope and crossed the brook, up a rock bank under a canopy of cottonwoods, then into a pasture that'd grown wild with disuse. The Hennekers, I believe, have more land than their cattle can manage for them. John needs to up his herd. Or let some bison in. Then again, I should not be so quick to advise un-asked, as much of my land to the west looks just the same as this. That pasture—though I guess it's really straight re-claimed prairie—ran all the way to the farmhouse. There were eventually beef cattle grazing who'd look at us curi-ously as we passed. Great black and crimson cows. The grass was shorter near the farm.

The younger two Henneker boys met us at the gate and took Ghost and Coyote into the barn, their little sister chas-ing along after. I believe she was intent on brushing them. It was beginning to make sense to me why John wanted his dam foaled so bad. A girl child had lit a fire under his ass for something pretty to ride. He didn't give a damn what kind of horse he fostered as long as it was a horse. I felt fine with my choice of sire. John Henneker came along a mo-ment later, worrying his fingers with a dirty red rag, then shook my hand and the boy's hand and admired the paint entirely on its color and shape. He did not look at its teeth, and I was glad. It's always a favor when folk don't pretend to know something. I explained to him the horse was not really a Paint, just painted. He looked at me like I was a moron. John's wife Evelyn came out after that and asked if we'd like something to eat or drink. We did. We had coffee and cold lunch in their kitchen and when we were done, we took the sire to a paddock where Henneker's bay draft horse Dilly was waiting. We let the two of them figure it out from there.

We stood there leaning against the wood fence, watching. Me and the boy and John Henneker and Evelyn. I was prepared to leave the paint for a day or more to give them time to adjust to one another, but they proved to make pretty fast friends. The two horses circled and sniffed each other, then the dam lifted her tail and pissed and the sire sniffed the piss, then sniffed its source and climbed on. He was a solid three hands shorter than she and just about fell off on his first attempt. But it's a lesson each of us eventually learns. It wasn't long before they got it all worked out.

John paid me after that. You could tell he'd made a special trip to the bank just for this. Crisp new bills still bound in a paper band. While we shook hands, John's youngest two—one boy and one girl—led out our rides by their bridles. Both horses looked well brushed. The girl was leading the boy's horse. She knew it. It pleased the boy and she knew that, too. We mounted then led the sire by his rope out the gate, and he seemed a little more frolicky than usual. The rutting has put some pep in him. Trotted out of the used pasture then galloped when we hit the disused part. Everyone seemed happy for the speed.

Heading back, we took a different route home. The sun was angling lower making everything bright green and golden. The horses shook their heads and made sounds, as if they found it pleasing to try an untrod path. Once on our own land, we cut southwest past the orchards into a pasture grown tall and wild. We rode until we reached our cold water pond, big flat rocks and silt at its edges. Narrow creek nuzzling out of the shallows, acting casual sneaking southwest to join up with its friends and rush wicked into the Missouri. In its middle, you could see the pond's face purling where the spring boiled up underneath. I can remember a time when the boy would ask where the water came from, how come it was always there. I know as much about it now as I did then. We tied the horses to a bone-dry and uprooted cottonwood root, then took off our clothes and swam. The boy was laughing. He could slice through the water like some silvery, brown-eyed fish. He did not learn this from me. I am all mammal in water, built to push through it, get to the other side. Have to remind myself that this is not a job. But the boy needs no reminding. Dive to the bottom and come up with rocks, little white twists that might be ancient bone. He's teaching me what is fun. I'd crouch in shallow water up to my chin and he'd balance his feet in the stirrup on my hands. Then I'd stand up quick, and launch him.

June 1st, 1965

Every morning, there's a great revival of birds singing all at once in the orchard trees and pastures. See them lined up on the crossbeams of our tin-can scarecrow in the garden. Watch them slice shapes in the air. They never stop singing when they fly. They will light on the backs of sleeping horses and sing. I do not know if they understand what the other birds are saying, or if they even understand themselves.

I have never known the name of any bird other than a crow. But the boy knows. He is learning. There's a library book with colored pictures, and a record of the songs they sing. It's one of the things he studies. He'll put on the record and page through the book. Our house filled with the songs of singing birds. He knows the names that people use and the Latin names used only by doctors and poets. He feels it is his inheritance and responsibility, the naming of all the birds when there's no one else here who can name them anymore.

June 2nd, 1965

Drove the boy to the library. He's a collector now of everything. Engine design and Iron Age wars and big books of maps, places I never heard of. Asked him on the ride home if he minded that I'd taken him out of school for so long. He said no, he didn't mind, but by fall he'll want to go back. He knows what this is about. I hope I'll be ready by then.

June 4th, 1965

Today came the man from the big Montana ranch with his two trucks hauling long gooseneck trailers. We had spoken on the phone. This was expected. Sort of waddled when he hopped down out of his truck, but the other driver didn't even turn off his engine. Without these deals now and then to big ranches, an operation small as ours would go under in a season. It saves us. Even still, it saddens me to see so many animals gone in one day. I feel a closeness to these things. Quarter horses and mules. Strange animals like great dogs with hooves, both sweet and wild. The Montanan had the specs of his order and it'd have been easy enough for the boy and I to gather in his horses—they are familiar with us and don't worry when we cull any one of them from the team—but the Montanan wanted to have a physical role in their selection. Which made it a true culling. They ran. We spent the morning chasing them in circles, cutting horses out one at a time. It was a waste of time, and it scared the beasts. But the Montanan felt very proud of his efforts and his active hand in the choosing. The work was a joy for him because it was his choice to work. The boy kept arrowing glances my way, like he wanted me to say something, stand up to this pot-bellied rich man. I couldn't rightly tell him then that this one sale would spell easy sailing for the rest of the year. So I held my tongue and cut the horses one by one and later forgot to explain. So I guess he still sees me more as a coward than a business man.

For letting him pretend he was a cowboy, the rancher threw in a bonus. Then he took his sixteen head of skittish horses and went back to Montana. The boy said he wished that lost sixteen luck. I take that to be his way of saying that he was not fond of the fat man. It was long after dark when what was left of my team finally lost fear and grew still.

June 5th 1965

I let the boy sleep more lately than I did when he went to school. There really isn't enough work now for two men. I can do the rote chores in the morning while he sleeps. Save the more interesting work to tackle later on as a team. But even with these dawn chores, I'm learning to take my time. This morning I went out onto the porch with my coffee, thinking I'd watch the blue world take on all its colors with the sun, but as soon as I stepped out, I saw on the deck boards a little grey lump. A big black beetle was rolling the lump around. Sometimes burying its head into a softness. And as it moved the lump around, I realized what I was seeing was a very small, very dead bird. I do not know what bird it was. It hadn't any feathers to speak of, just the moldy fuzz of a hatchling. The beetle unfolded the bird's bunched-up neck and articulated its clenched legs. I know the beetle was just feeding, but it seemed it was trying to reanimate the bird. As if by exercising its limbs, it could bring it back to life. I crouched there on the porch watching the beetle work to resuscitate this little rotten thing. Then I went back inside. Without my noticing, the blue of the world was gone.

But a curiosity was in me now. Took the little ash shovel down from its place by the wood stove and went back outside, scooped the bird and beetle up. Set them on a stump behind the house where I once had to cut an old rock elm down. Figured they'd be safe over there. Keep an eye on them now and then without worrying the boy might find them. I don't know how he'd react to this sort of thing. I'm not sure how I'm reacting myself.

June 6th, 1965

Thought I saw you hanging laundry today. Wind whipping the white sheets to snapping at your heels. But it was just the boy. Doing the job you used to do.

June 8th, 1965

The boy went out to pick alpine strawberries (or as my ma used to call them, *fraises des bois*) with the Hautenot girl this morning in the Kelloggs' fields south of here, so I took the truck into town. I needed nails and coffee and thought maybe I'd see what else they got at the store that we've never tried before. I think it's good for the boy to try new things. I do not like being in that house all alone. Went to the hardware store and got some nails and a new leather punch as mine has mysterious grown bent (a mystery I'm sure the boy knows the solution to) then talked to Henry for a spell and had an RC Cola because business was slow for Henry and I was in no hurry. He didn't have anything worth saying to say. At the Hy-Vee, got the coffee and a box of pancake mix because I can't make them right from scratch—there is something I'm missing that I cannot get right—and nothing else looked interesting so I bought a giant Southern watermelon. It was shaped like a box. I suspected the boy would get a kick out of that. The girl working checkout was pretty and smiled at me a lot. But I couldn't really smile back. I'm not ready yet for that kind of attention, it does no good for me now. So I didn't look at her at all. I hope she understands.

Driving home, waiting at a red light, I happened to notice a little orange butterfly flying circles round above the pavement. It was new tar macadam there. It was black. The butterfly kept circling the same patch of road like there was something there it liked. But there was nothing there. Then a worrying thing happened, as I started feeling a sort of panic tightening up in my throat. Just off the shoulder, there were flowers growing in the grass, and not far past that, fields of flowers. So why was this butterfly circling hot tar? Maybe there wasn't anything there where it was circling, but there used to be. Maybe it was remembering something that was long gone, paved over and buried. What I understand is that butterflies are always heading somewhere, either to or from some breeding ground in Mexico. But this one wasn't going anywhere. Just circling where something used to be. I was scared it might die by this choice. Get burned up on the sun-hot tar or hit any second now by a car. The world is too much for an animal so small to make choices that aren't only survival. The light had turned green but I hadn't noticed. Then someone behind me leaned on their horn. I wanted to save that stupid damn bug. But I couldn't. I couldn't even try. I drove through the light and brought the melon home to our boy.

June 10th, 1965

The dead bird moves a lot in the night. If it lay along the northeast rings of the stump at dusk, it'll be in the southern rings by morning. It's as if the beetle is passing coded messages, divining the weather, spelling good omens I hope. And too: there is a dead spider on the stump now as well. I don't know what killed either of these things. Only know they are gathering here.

June 13th, 1965

Ronald Haskell called about renting one of the mules to pull a load of wood he aims to fell in the back quarter of his property. Told him for an extra two hundred dollars, he could have a mule and keep it. It was a good deal for him, but I don't think he wanted it. I felt like a bully, sticking so firm to my offer. All mule or no mule. He came and got his animal before suppertime.

Later, the boy and I took Ghost and Coyote out in the west pastures. Sometimes trotting the horses and sometimes letting them run. It was aimless, the paths we took. Mostly let the beasts decide. The sky was liquid bright with colors but the dark lay low to the ground, almost black, everything just an outline of a shape. Shape of the boy. Shape of a tree. Far out, we saw some scavenger birds cutting circles in the air, so we rode out to see what we'd find. Dead doe splayed out in the grass, its hindquarters mostly ate off. A look of permanent terror fixed on its eyeless face. It stank. Ghost and Coyote stamped in the grass and threw their heads. They hated it.

Heading back, the boy pointed out the weather tower, getting taller. But I didn't want to see it. I spat.

June 14th, 1965

We were stripping an old saddle down to its tree when the boy asked me if we were ever going to talk about it. Didn't seem to me there was anything to talk about. But I didn't even say that. I showed him where the skirt tied into the tree. Then I cut the seam.

I believe he's beginning to resent me. He didn't like learning that Ron Haskell had taken the mule for keeps. He's been spending more time with the Hautenot girl. That scrawny whippet with all the teeth. Over dinner, he stressed to me how much he was looking forward to starting school again in the fall. We both pretended like school wasn't still in session for everybody other than him.

After the boy went to bed, I stood out in the yard awhile listening to the wind and the horses and the rattle of the tin cans hanging in the scarecrow and what I assume was an owl calling, though it wasn't how I imagine an owl ought to sound. Then I went inside and found a lantern and headed off west past the orchards, tall grass hushing around my knees. I did not light the lamp until I got to our pond. I followed the horse paths there. Took off my clothes and folded them and set them in a pile beside the lantern on a flat rock. Then I went for a swim. The half-moon was high and set the water sparkling and I swam to the far side and back three times and on the fourth pass stopped and tread water in the center. There was nothing else out there. Just me and the water and the moon and the lamp. The lamp was only there so I could find the shore again when I was done. You couldn't see the far hills. Just prairie in all directions forever. But nothing felt far away. It was all right there with me. In the water or close to shore. The moon and lantern and the cold spring beneath my feet. Everything right there with me. I stayed as long as the cold water would let me. Then I swam to the light and got dressed and walked home, the lantern now dark in my hand.

Across the distance, I saw the kitchen light was on. You were sitting at the table when I walked in, playing solitaire and drinking a glass of ginger ale in your hospital gown. It's the last thing I'd seen you wearing. Two moths fluttered about the yellow light above your head. There were eyes of wet on your glass. I smiled and took my boots off and said hello, and you smiled at me and waved and said nothing. Your skin was very grey but your eyes were still cool like wet slate. Mouth tight and twisted like you were holding back a laugh. You gathered the cards and shuffled. I found a dusty bottle of Canadian Club in a high cupboard shelf and poured myself a glass and poured a splash in yours. I sat across from you at the table and you dealt out the cards. I wanted very badly to touch you. Your blonde hair was stringy and kept falling in your face. I wanted to tuck it behind your ear, touch the hollow where your jaw bends to meet your neck. But I didn't. I knew that was against the rules. There were dark bruises inside your elbows and on the back of your hands where the IVs had gone in. There was still a paper bracelet around your narrow wrist. A bird's wrist. We played a few hands of Rummy, matching runs and pairs. Then you asked me where I've been and I told you I went for a swim in the pond. But you shook your head and said that's not what you meant. I could see your knee peeking beneath the edge of your hospital gown and without thinking reached to touch it with the tip of my finger, the acre of my palm, but you shook your head again. Then you were gone.

I sat for a long time in the kitchen beneath the moths spinning in the light, my hair still wet from the pond. It was cold. Even with the night still and the wind far away, this house creaks like old bones. The unseen motions of ancient things. I turned out the light and went to bed.

June 18th, 1965

The boy told me today that I am stupid for selling the mule. We were weeding our small garden, culling the little shoots of jewelweed and pigweed and plantain from among the potato mounds and pea vine and bush beans. He said that I was getting it all backward. Said we ought to have lent the mule to the Haskells for free as a favor, and only charged him if the beast got hurt or took ill. He insisted that favors are worth more than dollars, as the price of gold goes up and down but a favor is always a favor. At the very least, we should have traded services, as the Haskells raise good hay and oats, and they needed the mule to haul wood, all of which are things we will need come wintertime. But regardless: we should not have sold the mule.

I said to him that I suppose he thinks we ought to have let our paint rut with the Henneker's dray for free, too. And I should fix every saddle and bridle and harness for whoever comes begging at our door. He agreed the leatherwork ought to cost, but to charge to let an untested colt plow a draft horse for no other purpose than to make an animal whose only job will be to be an animal? He thought it was a pointless and mean thing, asking money for that.

I reminded him that what we ran was a horse farm. Then he did something that surprised me. He was squatting down in the potato mounds, but he'd stopped picking weeds. He was looking at his hands in the cool, dark earth. Then he said that people's sympathy for me was wearing thin. He said I was eating up our neighbors' goodwill by being a greedy fly.

I told him sympathy was another name for cancer. I'd be happier when it was gone.

The boy stood up and chucked a clod of rotten seed potato at me. It sailed over my shoulder and struck the line of tin cans strung to our scarecrow crucifix. Then he marched out of the garden. Headed south. I suspect to go play with that homely Hautenot girl.

I finished weeding my row of peas. I worked in the barn on a new bridle and traces set. I stood in the orchard and listened to the nicker of horses, the scream of birds. I did not go into the house. I stood with the wind pushing my

141

shoulders and tugging at my clothes. Then I got into the truck and drove. I didn't go anywhere. There was nowhere I wanted to go. I drove the dirt roads between farms and fields and looked out at the cattle standing still and chewing. I watched the sun melt off in the hills and the silver flint of moon rise up. Stars and the occasional mercury lamp burning cold over a closed barn door. I drove until very late before turning and heading back. I could smell the sweet dust gusting off the road as I passed along. Hoped the boy would be home when I got there.

June 20th, 1965

Afternoon clouds got dark all at once and a warm wind blew in hard and wet from the south. An uneasiness breathed in by the weather. I'd been sleeping but something woke me. Like a cool hand tracing down my neck. Looked to see what it was but saw nothing. Then I saw what was happening outside. Looked for the boy but could not find him so called but he wouldn't call back. The scarecrow's tin cans banged together like the drums in an Indian's dance. In the pastures, the horses were running hard, making noise, being beasts. The mules faced the wind and were mules. I saddled Circle as she hadn't been rode in some time and took to the fallow pastures at a steady beat and found the boy up in a box elder southwest of the farm. It was a squat arthritis tree with the pale undersides of its leaves turned up. It was the only tree around. Just a lot of tall grass lying flat beneath the wind. The boy's face was all wet and he wouldn't look at me. This was nothing I'd thought him liable to still do, to runaway and to cry. I wasn't sure how to react to that. I did not like him in the tree. As he was on a low branch and I was on your horse, we were just about on a level with each other. I reached out and patted his shoulder. But I felt like a little league coach doing that, consoling a batter after striking out on an unimportant play. I suspected that sentiment was incorrect. He didn't look hurt, so I assumed it must be the other thing. The wind was getting worse and there was some deep animal sound coming from the clouds. It was a mean thing to say, but I told him to stop that now. Then I reached out and put an arm behind his back and pulled him onto Circle ahead of me on the saddle. He was too old for that kind of thing. But we had to move. I put the heels to your horse and we rode hard and fast back to the house. The quarter horses were acting like horses again, calm with the wind whipping back their mane. The jack donkey was chewing oats. They didn't care. They could handle themselves. We disrobed Circle and set her and Ghost and Coyote loose in the pasture with the others. Three white horses among varnished sorrels and blue roans and charcoal blacks underneath an evil marble of storm. Then we went inside, and first it hailed but then it rained in dark ribbons so you could see it wind like snakes through the air while far to the south, though we couldn't tell how far, we watched a black tornado touchdown and ride.

June 21st, 1965

The bird is less lump and more skeleton now. No sign of the beetle. Where'd he go?

June 22nd, 1965

A full month or more after all the others had passed, the last late dam foaled today. I'm sure she had her reasons, but as they're horse reasons, I wasn't made privy. The boy'd been feeding sugar cubes to the quarter horses when he saw what was happening and ran back to the house. In his excitement, he forgot he wasn't talking to me. Put in the call to Dr. Vining, then saddled Ghost and Coyote and culled the dam real easy from the team. Put her in a paddock behind the stables. There was just a pale blue bubble like a misplaced balloon swelling out from her sex. But in the balloon there were hooves. She circled once slowly the paddock's dusty edge then lay herself down in the shade.

It wasn't much longer after that and with little more to do but to watch. Dr. Vining showed up and waved his hat and took up alongside us at the fence. Had only called him in in case there was trouble with the afterbirth. There weren't. The dam passed the foal and licked off its blue membrane then passed the afterbirth and ate that too. She nuzzled the foal until it found its feet and wobbled and had its first feeding. The dam was all chestnut with white showing on her ribs but the foal was buckskin, pale on its underside with a diamond between its eyes. After it fed, it gamboled a bit, ungainly but excited like it'd been looking forward to this chance to finally stretch out.

Dr. Vining refused any payment. Said he was happy to have been useless in the presence of such an easy birth. An uncommon twitchiness meanwhile was torturing the boy. He does not normally get worked up over new foals, but today on all accounts seems is an exception. Said he'd like to ride out and fetch his friend, the Hautenot girl, as to show her the new foal. So maybe his excitement was on loan from her. Girls and horses. As she'd be riding back with him, I suggested he bring Circle along. They'd then each have their own ride. This seemed to please him, too. I hope he remembers this, that I am not always so contempt-ible. Saddled up Circle and mounted Coyote and took off with both horses across the southern fields. Watching them go, Dr. Vining laughed and said what a hell of a boy and I laughed with him and agreed, though I could only suspect what the doctor was commenting on. It didn't matter. Maybe I was starting to feel some of this contagious animal excitement as it was with a sudden burst of good feeling that I asked the doctor if he'd like to stick around for a spell, have a coffee or take a quick ride. Said he wished he could but duty called. He did not say what duty, though. He said my name and started his pickup and in a moment he was gone and very suddenly the farm felt emptied. I was still smiling in the yard but there was nothing to smile at. All at once, I was alone.

Went and checked on the foal and dam and found them sleeping in the dust, bellies rising big with deep, sleepy breaths. It's always made me uneasy, seeing horses sleeping but not standing, lying on the ground like they're dead. In the pasture, the mules and horses had gathered as close as they could to watch. Looked at their black eyes all pointed at me and could not know what they saw. Walked through the stables, sweet with the faint hay and manure smells but vacant for the summer so feeling abandoned and forgot. The few slit-eyed barn cats here and there did not ease this deserted feeling. My brief flash of excitement was gone. People take it with them when they go. Stood out in the dooryard looking west, wondered what to do with myself while I waited, saw the weather tower far out and almost complete putting its mark on the horizon, and a stomach-sour anger took me. I'm sick of that thing and it has only just arrived. My feeling anything won't make it go away.

Keys were in the house but there's a spare in the shop. Started the truck and drove south to the first crossroad. Drove west.

The tower was farther out than I expected. Seemed it got bigger the longer I drove but not any closer. That worsened the sourness in me. Forty or fifty miles out, hit a crossroad where I could see more traffic had been going—there was caked mud and dust on the pavement—so turned in that direction and soon found a dirt scratch cutting through the prairie toward the tower. From the road I could see two cranes and a job trailer and all these stacks of material, and it was all up on a small rise but when I got there, there were no men working. The site was empty. Just machines and material. Got out the truck and took a few steps toward the thing. Then I just kind of stood there. It was likely two hundred feet tall. Just four long legs and metal Xs zipping up in between. It looked like it should all lead up to something. But at the top, there was just a red glass lantern. Like a lighthouse in the prairie.

I stood there a while feeling helpless. Scooped up a rock and threw it, but the rock sailed right through, missing the legs and braces and landing in the dirt with a poof. I suppose this is what impotence feels like. They take everything away and bury it behind some church somewhere and leave you nothing but the world stretching wide all around you. But they won't even leave you that. They build a lighthouse where there is no water, just something to remind you that even this they've taken away. You can't even look upon a goddamn sunset without being reminded of some lost time that was better. It grants no mercy to us trying to forget.

I do not remember driving home. The boy and his ugly girl were fawning over the foal. They waved when they seen I was back. Somehow, seeing that made everything worse. Went into the workshop and for the first time in years, shut the door.

June 23rd, 1965

Over dinner asked the boy if he'd like to ride the fences with me and repair what needed repairing. Not just the far-side of the orchards. The whole back forty. The boundary lines and interior partitions. We could harness a mule and load the cart with new fence posts and boards. We could pack tools and food and bedrolls, take it easy and camp out when we had a mind to. Take a few days. Make an adventure out of it. I asked him if he'd like that. But he didn't say anything.

I told him the best thing to do when you see a rattlesnake is to pretend you don't see a rattlesnake. Just walk the other way. Let it be. I asked him, does that make sense?

I waited for him to answer. Then I told him: we are going to repair the fences. We will harness a mule and load the cart with provisions. We will work as a team and sleep in the fields. I didn't try to make it sound fun this time. Made it sound like the work it was. I asked him, did he understand?

The boy responded with a very slow nod. When I asked him to say it, he said he understood. There wasn't any life in his voice or in his eyes. He stared at his plate awhile then got up and left the room. He put on his record of bird songs.

He does not understand yet that a kind person can be hard sometimes and still not be a mean person. Just as a cruel person can sometimes grant favors and still not be generous. All he sees is me being firm or silent or pushing, and that makes me a bully or greedy or unfeeling. He isn't curious about the why. Or he's already made up his mind. And what he's made up is wrong. If it was just me here now, I wouldn't give a damn. I'd likely let all the horses go and get wild on their own. Or I would lead them to some-place greater than this. Take nothing else and ride north. Manitoba or Saskatchewan. What we think is big is small up there. What we call empty is full. I would lead the horses until they chose to lead themselves, tear their hooves away from me in some unending Canadian prairie. I would leave them and ride up where I could be so small that I wouldn't even exist. That would be a solution to all things.

It is for the boy that I do not do that. Instead, I do eve-rything else. He's too much of a child to understand.

June 24th, 1965

I have let the issue of repairing the fence slide.

The boy's gone over to the Hautenot's for supper. He still is not talking to me. He's taken Coyote along but it's a long pasture ride to take in the dark. I do not suspect he will be back tonight. I had hoped this time would bring us clos-er together. I know, it is something we both need now. A proximity not just of flesh. But I feel instead that we're driven apart. There is no question that I am to blame. He

148

sees me as stubborn and maybe a little cold in my heart. How can I know if he's wrong? With only two of us here, there is nothing else to contrast me to, no other voice to provide context. And maybe I am different now. In our solitude, I've become something I was not before. I would not need defending if it weren't just he and I. There'd be nothing to defend. I hope in his adulthood he does not look back on me with resentment and disappointment. I would rather he hate me, as hate is close to love. But disappointment is an open gate to not caring. I do not want him to learn to not care about his father. But he probably will.

Alone, I saw no point in cooking supper. I worked on a saddle the Fensters had left me to repair. I checked in on the beetle and spider and bird. When the sun was aiming to set, I headed westward from the house, just so far as to put the orchard at my back. I wanted an unimpeded view of the grasses and far hills and the sun. The clouds spread the light around so the whole sky was hot and waxy. There was wind. There came a point when everything was red. The sun red. The prairie red. The Missouri River which I cannot see and the faraway hills and the Bad Lands all red as a liquid and beating heart. In the weather tower, now complete, a single red light. If I looked at my hands, they'd have been red too. But I did not look at myself.

I asked if you were far away.

You said, "I am."

I asked if I was making a mistake.

You said I am.

But you would not tell me what it was.

I know there will be a time when this distance is not so great. When I am allowed to touch you again. But that time is so far away. I asked if I would get this right but already, you were gone behind the hills, and everything in the world was blue.

June 25th, 1965
    The bird and beetle are gone.

"Blue of the World" was written as part of a fellowship with the Hewnoaks Artists Colony.

Out of the Bag

by Sally J. Pla

Maybe they don't notice, she thinks. Because childhood's flawless default is love and trust, evidenced in the dog-like devotion of her puppy-pack of boys. Love and trust. Maybe they don't actually absorb any of this.

Besides, since their father's been sick, he's been better. He's physically around, for one thing. He notices them, smiles at their endless clatter, their chatter, their bluster. He is standing in the kitchen, right now: a careful side-part drawn through the comb-toothed ridges of the sparse new hair coming in, baby-fine and unnatural grey. He is aromatic of soap and medication, with a face as pale as a bar of Ivory. He stares into the coffee mug clasped in his bony hand this Saturday morning. He is physically around, now that he's sick, so she takes this as a brand-new package, brand-new story. She whips him up fresh, along with the pancake batter.

"Here's your sleepy old daddyo, come to play! Why don't you take him out to the yard. Shoo, the bunch of

151

you!" she sings from the stove. "Go on outside until I call you."

The boys, a mini-tornado, rip through the room.

"Go on," she urges him in a different voice, removing his cup, then standing on tiptoe behind him and raising her hand until it hovers, flat and open, a half-inch from the skin of his back, not daring to touch. On either side of her outstretched hand, his shoulder blades protrude through his tee shirt like folded dragon wings. His mouth, once beaked and sharp, sputters ashy protests.

"Go on," she goads with syrupy cheer. He drops his head.

She turns back to the pancakes. Steam, yeast, and vanilla rise from the pan with familiar reassurance. Behind her, she hears the screen door click shut—then there he is, through the window, looking uncertain. He decides to go pull weeds from the flowerbed, while the boys shout and run nearby. He's missing the roots.

*

That screen door. That screen. She stares at it, remembering how it got shredded to bits on the day that everything changed for them. It was last year, midsummer, and he was out after work as usual, while she and the boys were home.

The dog had erupted from the blue midnight silence into a howling, bow-yowling, moon-mad frenzy, like to raise the dead. And she flew downstairs to get hold of him. Holding tight to his collar, she'd peered out across the lawn. What did that old hound sense? Prowlers? Or him? Or worse: Him and his friends.

She strained to hear—what?

Then she looked down.

In a pool of yellow porch-light, on the back step, she noticed an empty Wise Potato Chip bag.

She blocked the dog's frantic nose with her knee, and cracked the door for a better look. The bag was alive. It rustled all on its own, then jerked sideways. She slammed the door, but stayed put, breathing heavy through the screen at the unnatural sight.

A tip of dark tail unfurled luxuriously from the opening.

Skunk? Cat? Rabid raccoon?

The dog exploded into a second frenzy of barks, pawing at the door, frantic. White bits of foamy slobber flew wild off his jowls.

She stepped back. She didn't need any fresh absurdity. She wanted to close her eyes and go back to sleep, put the pillow over her head and pretend that nothing bewildering ever darkened her doorstep.

But now the little boys were arriving, slumping down the stairs yawning, their eyebrows curving into sideways question marks.

"It's nothing," she said. "Everything's fine. Go back to bed." With a hand on the dog's collar, she reopened the door just enough to poke at the bag with a toe.

"Mom!" said the oldest. "What is it?" Then they all chanted in. "What is it?" "What is it?"

Her heart thumped. Something had to happen. Just, something had to. *Had to.* Something, anything.

"Okay, stand back," she said. Then, holding her breath, in one sweeping motion, she whipped the bag up and off whatever mysterious Thing was lurking in it. She slammed the screen door and froze behind it. Her heart felt like it was punching its way right out of her chest.

Something black somersaulted through a spray of crumbs and landed on all fours. Then it glared at her, claws splayed, back hunched, its eyes like giant yellow sparks in a muscular skull of coal-colored velvet. It hissed.

She stared; it stared back.

The wind died; the dog's barks faded out of her brain. Time stopped. It was just her and this tiny panther, together in silent porch-light communion.

What did you expect to see? The creature's eyes locked onto her. *What did you expect?*

She and the cat stayed like that for an eon, through the history of time.

Then, shaky headlights beamed into the gravel drive.

"Mom!" the boys whispered, excited, behind her.

"It's nothing," she said. "Just some house cat." She watched as the creature shot across the lawn into the fulminating dark.

"No, Mom! Look!" They pointed downward. The dog, frantic during all this, had apparently shredded the bottom of the screen in the door into absolute fringe. She hadn't even noticed.

A year later, it's still hanging like that. Something in her doesn't want to fix it.

*

The boys are getting big. They always loved the silly, exciting version she told them of the Night of the Cat. They loved it from the very first. They made her tell it for the first time just moments after it happened, when their father came in, shaking, pale as ash and salty with a sick, unnatural sweat. Home early, sick, and sober.

The boys had laughed, oblivious to the whole wide world, and jumped up and down. "Tell him, Mama!" they said. "Daddy's home! Tell him how you let that cat out of the bag!"

She'd smiled brightly, taken a deep breath, and started in.

With Baby Wynona
by Cady Vishniac

Baby Wynona's strapped to my chest with a Moby we got from our Head Start nurse, but then she squirms one stubby arm free and reaches for the butterfly. "Red," she says. "God, so perfectly red. Like a fire engine." We're at the Franklin Park Conservatory. Mike, my manager at the convenience store by the university, is sweet on me, so he bought the ticket.

I stifle a yawn. "Wynnie, honey, that's a Double-Banded Judy. Its Latin name is abisara bifasciata."

"I can read the sign." She kicks my ribs.

"Good," I say in my best mom voice, "because the sign also says not to touch anything."

Wynona rolls her eyes, grabs the pacifier I keep clipped to my shirtfront, and sucks on it greedily. Then she spits the thing out again. "That guy keeps staring at you. Don't look."

I look. There's a man behind us with his brown hair in a ponytail, his gnarled feet in leather sandals. He has a Portuguese Water Dog on a footlong lead. I don't think dogs are allowed in here, but then again, nobody's stopping him.

Wynona kicks me again."He's cute, right?"

The man is cute, in a hippie way, but I haven't bathed in days and my bra is crusted with leaky breast milk. I doubt he'd be interested in me.

I ask Wynona, "What do you think of Mike?" because Mike definitely is interested. The other day, he met my eye over the rows of corn chips and beef jerky and told me I owe Wynona a father. I've been thinking about it. I don't feel any attraction to Mike, but a father could drive us places, or play with Wynona while I bake lasagna, or hand her a bottle when she wakes up in the middle of the night screaming, the way she did last night. If Mike had been around, I could have gotten some rest.

"What do I think of Mike?" Wynona cranes her neck to meet my eyes. "You mean your boss? I think if he ever asked you out, that would be sexual harassment." Then she puts her pacifier back in and looks, pointedly, at a cluster of pupating danaus plexippus, monarchs, gold dots on their neon green cocoons.

It's ten minutes, maybe. Longer than her attention span is supposed to last. Longer than mine does. I am, in fact, fed up with the bright insects, the dappling sunlight, the pleasant shrubs and pots of milkweed, so I make my way in the direction of the greenhouse exit. I want to catch the origami exhibit—the paper cranes with wingspans wider than I am tall, the herd of multicolored paper horses—then go home and put Wynona down for her afternoon nap. If I'm lucky this can be my nap, too.

Except Wynona hates my plans, all of them. "Don't you dare leave," she says. "They release the painted ladies in three minutes. If we're gone before then, I'll puke on your chest." She makes hurking noises to prove she's serious, but stops when she sees the cute hippie and his dog have crept up next to us.

The hippie taps my shoulder. "Did I hear your baby talking?"

Wynona's turned to the employees-only side door through which, I guess, she expects the painted ladies to arrive. Her body jiggles. I can barely keep my eyes open. My ankles ache.

"Babies don't talk." I gape at the hippie like he's out of his mind.

"My mistake," he says.

A fresh-faced assistant, a college girl, wheels through the door with a mesh cage, transparent chrysalides hanging from the top. Wynona digs her fingernails into my collar-bone. A couple other families are in here with us, grandparents and aunts and uncles and cousins and babysitters. We all gather in a circle around the cage, and the assistant starts her spiel. "Good morning. I'm so glad you've all come to watch my friends here emerge," and so on.

It takes a whole hour for all the painted ladies to rip through the chrysalides. Wynona is rapt for the painfully slow process. I'd be bored, if I weren't so focused on staying awake. Watching each lady uncrinkle her feelers and spread her wings and flutter and fall and flutter and fall and flutter and fall and flutter and finally stay airborne is only a little bit better than watching paint dry.

"Time to go free." The assistant slides open the top of the cage and the ladies stream forth. Wynona gasps. She is, I think, grateful I brought her here, and in exchange for her gratitude I won't even mind that we have zero time left for the origami.

We stand in place while the ladies swirl in the air around us, alighting in the corner on a yellow-flowering tree.

The other children, their families, the hippie, and his dog file out.

Wynona squirms her arm free again, then the other arm, then hugs my neck. She whispers in my ear, "Before we leave, you should know: I'm soaked with piss."

So it's an emergency change under the yellow lights of Conservatory bathroom, then we walk to the bus stop. But we only make it as far as the parking lot. The hippie is there, tossing a frisbee. His dog catches the frisbee in rubbery lips and runs in a circle before dropping it at the hippie's feet. Toss and catch. Circle. Drop.

The hippie looks over at Wynona. "Wanna say hi?" His ears stick out in an endearing way.

So I unwrap Wynona from her Moby and hold her up under the armpits. She takes several shaky, non-weight-bearing steps toward the dog, which licks her with its black tongue.

She shrieks, saliva coating her face. She laughs my favorite laugh.

We've been out of the house for almost three hours now. I feel grimy. Nap is going to be late, but what can I do? I pull an old towel from the diaper bag and lay it on the hardtop, then I lay Wynona on the towel on her stomach so the dog can sniff her butt and whine at her and try to give her the frisbee.

Wynona giggles, but in-between giggles she has the presence of mind to whisper to me, "Talk to him. Please."

The hippie and I pull back to watch our charges play. I don't talk.

"Mike," he tells me. He reaches out his hand, and I almost don't shake it. I almost don't remember shaking hands is something human beings do. All I do these days is Wynona and work.

"I know a Mike," I say.

"Yeah? He your boyfriend?"

I see where this is going, but on second thought, I'm too tired to care. Maybe Hippie Mike is cuter than Boss Mike, but so what? It's not like I can date. It's not like I can trust this guy to help me out with Wynona when he's so young, as young as me, and he can't even wear real shoes in this late-autumn chill. So I tell Hippie Mike the other Mike isn't just my boyfriend, but my husband, Wynona's father. I make him a Marine for good measure, and I'm satisfied to see Hippie Mike's eyebrows shoot up like he knows he made a mistake.

I pick up Wynona and say it was nice to meet him, and Hippie Mike doesn't try to shake my hand again. I feel all right about it, but then, on the COTA bus home, Wynona gets mean. "What was that?" she says. "If you date your boss, I'll pee on you."

"You already peed on me," I say, shifting in the hard plastic seat. "But fine, I won't date my boss ... *if* you let me catch two whole hours of shut-eye." It's a desperate bargain, but I'm fading fast. I don't even know how I'll walk from the bus to our apartment.

"Done." A string of drool runs down Wynona's chin. "But why did you run away from that man and his cool dog? I'm worried about you. Who are you supposed to love?"

"You." I wipe the drool with my sleeve. "I'll just love you."

"That's mushy," she says. "And an awful lot of responsibility. Are you sure I'm up to it?" But she doesn't stop me as I blow in her ears. Just yawns and curls up in her Moby, sticks her butt out and her face in my cleavage, and succumbs to the lullaby of the bus engine, its soothing vibrations.

I arch my neck, stretching it over the steel bar of the seat, and look out the window. I'm not focusing on anything in particular. Columbus whizzes by, church moms in their minivans, a gaggle of shirtless hicks on dirt bikes, frat boys in their busted pickups and frat girls in their flashy red BMWs. The stadium and the science museum, pizza and florists and hipster cafes. It's all a blur.

Contributors

Jen Bergmark has published fiction in *Bellevue Literary Review*, *Indiana Review*, *Harpur Palate*, *Cream City Review*, *Puerto del Sol*, and elsewhere, and was anthologized in *New California Writing* (Heyday Books). She was a Poets & Writers Magazine California Exchange Award finalist, received the John Gardner Memorial Prize for Fiction, and has been a resident at Dorland Mountain Arts Colony and KHN Center for the Arts.

Anna Bernstein is a research assistant specializing in women's history. Her fiction has appeared in *Litro NY* and *deComP magazinE*, and her poetry in *Dunes Review*, *Inch*, *apt*, *Concho River Review*, and others. She recently won an International Publication Award from *Atlanta Review*.

Bethany Bowman teaches ESL at Taylor University. Her poems have appeared in *Apple Valley Review*, *Ascent*, *The Comstock Review*, *Midwestern Gothic*, and *Nimrod*, among others.

Kari Gunter-Seymour's chapbook *Serving* was chosen runner up in the 2016 Yellow Chair Review Annual Chapbook Contest and nominated for an Ohioana Award (Crisis Chronicles Press 2018). Her poems can be found in *Rattle, Crab Orchard Review, Stirring,* and on her website karigunterseymourpoet.com. She is an Instructor in the E.W. Scripps School of Journalism at Ohio University and Poet Laureate for Athens, Ohio.

A former English teacher, Maurine Haltiner lives in Salt Lake City, where she is a member of the Utah State Poetry Society.

Andrea Hansell earned a creative writing certificate at Princeton University and a Ph.D. in Clinical Psychology at the University of Michigan. Her essays and memoir pieces have appeared in *Lilith, Intima, DaCunha Global, Easy Street,* and elsewhere. Her short stories have appeared in *The Lascaux Review* and the *Ink Stains Anthology.*

Jackleen Holton's work has been published in the anthologies *The Giant Book of Poetry,* and *Steve Kowit: This Unspeakably Marvelous Life,* and has appeared or is forthcoming in journals including *Atlanta Review, Bellingham Review, North American Review, Poet Lore,* and *Rattle.*

David Jauss is the author of four collections of short stories, including *Glossolalia: New & Selected Stories* and the AWP Award-winning *Black Maps,* two volumes of poetry, and the essay collection *On Writing Fiction.* His stories have appeared in the *Best American Short Stories, O. Henry Prize,* and *Pushcart Prize* anthologies as well as *The Pushcart Book of Short Stories: The Best of the Pushcart Prize*. He teaches in the MFA in Writing Program at Vermont College of Fine Arts.

Lois P. Jones has work appearing or forthcoming in *Terrain* (two works as finalist judged by Jane Hirshfield), *Tinderbox Poetry Journal*, *Narrative*, *American Poetry Journal*, *Tupelo Quarterly*, *The Warwick Review*, and elsewhere. She is a winner of the Tiferet Poetry Prize, the Lascaux Poetry Prize, and the Bristol Poetry Prize, and is a multiple Pushcart nominee. Lois is poetry editor at *Kyoto Journal*, host of KPFK's Poets Café (Pacifica Radio), and co-host of Moonday Poetry in La Cañada, California. Her first collection of poems, *Night Ladder*, was Glass Lyre Press's 2017 Editor's Choice.

Erica Plouffe Lazure's flash fiction collection, *Heard Around Town*, won the 2014 Arcadia Fiction Chapbook Prize. Her fiction has appeared in *McSweeney's Quarterly Concern*, *The Greensboro Review*, *Meridian*, *American Short Fiction*, *Fiction Southeast*, and elsewhere. She lives and teaches in Exeter, NH.

Douglas W. Milliken is the author of the novels *To Sleep as Animals* and *Our Shadows' Voice*, the collection *Blue of the World*, and several chapbooks, including *The Opposite of Prayer*. His stories have been honored by the Maine Literary Awards, the Pushcart Prize, and *Glimmer Train*, as well as published in dozens of journals, including *Slice*, *The Collagist*, and *The Believer*.

Karla K. Morton has published twelve poetry collections. Her work has appeared in *American Life in Poetry*, *Alaska Quarterly Review*, *Southword Journal*, and *The Comstock Review*. She is currently on her "Words of Preservation: Poets Laureate National Parks Tour" visiting all 60 National Parks. A percentage of sales from the forthcoming book will go back to the Parks System to help culturally preserve the next 100 years of the Parks.

George Petty's poems have appeared in *Water-Stone*, *Two-Rivers Review*, *Blueline*, *The Comstock Review*, *Sow's Ear Poetry Review*, and other journals, and have aired on National Public Radio. Some of his poems have been collected in a chapbook titled *Boulder Field*, from Finishing Line Press.

Sally J. Pla is the author of several books for young people: *The Someday Birds*, *Stanley Will Probably Be Fine*, and *Benji, The Bad Day, & Me.* Her writing for grown-ups has appeared most recently in *The Lascaux Review*. She lives in Southern California.

Karen Pojmann is a writer, editor and communications director living in Columbia, Missouri. Her poems have been published or are forthcoming in *Literary Mama*, *Helen*, *Writer's Digest*, *The Madison Review*, *Belletrist*, and *Mom Egg Review*.

Betsy Porter lives and writes near Portland, Oregon. Her stories have been published in *The Timberline Review* and performed by Liar's League.

Jessamine Price is a poet, essayist and teacher with an MFA from American University and an M.Phil. in history from Oxford. Her poems and essays have appeared in publications such as *Hunger Mountain*, *Rust + Moth*, and *Rattle*, and she was the winner of the Global Commemoration of Nanjing poetry contest judged by Grace Cavalieri. She currently teaches English in South Korea.

Tim Rolands's poems have been published in *Paintbrush: A Journal of Poetry and Translation* as well as *The New Press Literary Quarterly*. He has served as poetry editor at Truman State University Press and edited *Cat's Ear Poetry & Fiction*. He studied creative writing at Truman State University and now lives in central Wisconsin.

Michelle Ross is the author of *There's So Much They Haven't Told You*, winner of the 2016 Moon City Press Short Fiction Award. Her writing has appeared or is forthcoming in *Colorado Review*, *The Common*, *Gulf Coast*, *Electric Literature's Recommended Reading*, *TriQuarterly*, and other venues. She lives in Tucson, Arizona.

Kari Shemwell was born and raised in western Kentucky. She studied creative writing at Murray State University and recently graduated with an MFA degree from Sierra Nevada College. She now lives in New Orleans and works in the film industry. Her work has previously been published in

Stonecoast Review, The Masters Review, Gulf Stream Magazine, and *Berfrois.*

Maureen Sherbondy's latest collection is *Belongings.* She teaches English at Alamance Community College in Graham, NC.

K. J. Stevens earned an MFA from Lindenwood University. His work has been published in *The Adirondack Review, Temenos, Great Lakes Review, December Magazine,* and elsewhere.

Marilyn L. Taylor, former Poet Laureate of the state of Wisconsin and the city of Milwaukee, is the author of six poetry collections. Her poems and essays have appeared in *Poetry, American Scholar, Measure, Able Muse, Poemeleon,* and elsewhere, and the Penguin-Random House *Everyman's Anthology of Villanelles.*

Several of Rebecca Timson's plays have been produced in youth and community theaters. Recently her poems have been long-listed for the University of Canberra International Poetry Prize.

Anne Vetter is an artist and writer living in the Bay Area. Her work has appeared in *The Washington Post* and *Grimiore Magazine.*

Cady Vishniac is an Endelman/Gitelman fellow at the University of Michigan. Her stories have been published most recently in *Glimmer Train, New England Review,* and *New*

Stories from the Midwest, where she won the Jay Prefontaine Prize for Fiction.

Billie Girl, Vickie Weaver's first novel, won the 2009 Leapfrog Literary Press Fiction Award. Other honors include second place in the Twisted Road Southern Gothic Fiction Contest, winner of the Lush Triumphant Contest, and semi-finalist in the Mary McCarthy Prize. Her short stories have appeared in many literary journals and anthologies.

Jess Williard's poems have recently appeared or are forthcoming in *Third Coast, North American Review, Colorado Review, Southern Humanities Review, Sycamore Review,* and other journals. He lives in Atlanta where he is a doctoral candidate at Georgia State University.